Jantid

Abomination of Chernobyl

by

D.P. Pankratz

D.P. Pankratz

Jantid is a work of fiction, based off the April 26, 1986
Chernobyl meltdown in reactor #4. Names, characters, and places
used within the storyline are either, fictitious, or real places. Any
other events are a product of the imagination of the author.

Published in the United States by Lulu.com
LIBRARY AND ARCHEIVES CATALOGING-IN-
PUBLICATION DATA
Pankratz, Perry (Perry P.)
Jantid/D.P. Pankratz

ISBN 978-1-9994821-6-9

Printed in the United States of America
Lulu.com

Cover art by Simone Catherine Green @ Art in Insanity

First Edition

<u>Dedications</u>

To my loving wife Teresa, every new book is a lengthy part of our lives, souls, and more embedded in the pages within. Our love will live on forever, into the next world... love you!

Amanda Williams, a great editor who took up the challenge to help me get Jantid out onto the world... thank you!

Simone Catherine Green, an amazing lady with jaw dropping artwork. Thank you for drawing Jantid for me, you're the best!

I would also like to thank those who've stood by me in the darkest of times. Those of you who knew I needed a friend without me saying a word, friends like that are hard to come by... thank you!

I would also like to thank anyone I may have missed. Thank you!

April 26, 1986. A day the visible world changed forever. The Chernobyl nuclear reactor went into meltdown. Fear and panic engulf the world, not knowing what would happen tomorrow? Jade Mills, a newly graduated Marine Biologist who receives a phone the same day as the meltdown. A few hours later, finding herself on a plane destined for Russia. Upon arriving at an unknown checkpoint location, Jade and her fellow colleagues are led blindfolded into a foreign facility. A wafting smell of chemicals burns their noses as they enter.

Hundreds of men/women screaming and shouting indiscriminately, as Jade is led to a solitary room. Taking the blindfold off, forced to strip naked, she is given a decontamination shower. The cold water makes Jade shiver uncontrollably as she is scrubbed raw. After getting out, she is wrapped with a towel, and rushed to another room. She is given a hazmat suit to put on, and a sheet containing instructions where to go after she is suited up.

Three hours later, Jade stands with one-hundred other men, and women. People from every corner of the world. A man in a U.S. Army uniform walks to the forefront of the room. Stopping, as he turns and glares throughout the room cautiously before placing his hands behind his back. As everyone stares at him, waiting to say something, he finally states sternly,

Jantid

"Welcome to your home for the next six months to a year. I'm General Hera! You are the elite of your countries divisions. Some of you are biologists, scientists, while others are radiation specialists. If I have forgotten any fields, I'm sorry, but time is limited. As you've been informed, the Chernobyl plant went into meltdown at 1:23 A.M. Yesterday morning. This plant is still spewing radioactive isotopes along with other material into the atmosphere. You will be assigned into groups in accordance with what skill level you have been marked as. The Russian government doesn't know we are here. You are NOT to talk with any of the locals, just get in, grab samples, and get out again."

General Hera, pauses as he is given a piece of paper. After staring at it for a while, he continues talking,

"Your suits have a number assigned on them… each number represents a group. Each group is preassigned to a particular area in the hot zones. Those with the numbers one through six. You're the ones who are in the five-mile zone. Seven through twelve. You're in the twenty-mile zone. Thirteen through fifteen. You're in the fifty-mile zone. One through six. You will be closely monitored, and your job is going to be the most excruciating. You are tasked with getting water samples, and any living animal. Your time will be limited to five minutes on each rotation, any longer, and your safety from the radiation cannot be guaranteed. God be with you all!"

Jade watches as the General walks out of the room quickly, turning to her left, seeing the number two on her arm as she mutters,

"Damn."

The young man next to Jade replies,

"Could be worse… could be one of those poor fish that are going to grow extra parts."

Jade snickers as he holds his hand out and exclaims,

"Hi, I'm Lyle! Appears we are headed to the same place, I have the mark of two on my arm. I doubt any of the higher numbers want to change up numbers? Ha-ha!"

Jade can't help but let out a giggle as she answers,

"You have quite the sense of humor going into this. You doing drugs? Ha-ha!"

Lyle grins as he answers smitten.

"Well, I'm flabbergasted. Drugs, no! Just trying to make the best of the worst possible situation. Would you like to get a cup of coffee before we start growing extra arms, and I say arms because the likelihood of me growing elsewhere isn't going to happen? Ha-ha!"

Jade giggles again slapping Lyle's arm lightly, as Lyle holds his hand towards the nearby door. The two of them chatter away laughing away, as they walk down the hallway to the mess hall. As they sit next to each other, a hardened bond begins forming between the two.

An hour later, they're riding in self-contained trucks, heading towards the Chernobyl plant. Hours later, their truck comes to a stop. Everyone stares out the window, seeing smoke cascading out of the reactor through a huge hole in the side. A commander walks from the front of the truck, stopping in front of the twelve men and women sitting in the back. He sighs, staring at his clipboard, glancing up at them. After a few moments, he begins making marks on the board before stating,

Jantid

"Well, we're in the red-hot zone. The vehicle is the only barrier between us and the radiation. You will go in groups of two, and this device hanging over there. That is a Giger counter. One will carry that with them at all times if that little birdy starts to click rapidly, and that needle goes across the board, you get the hell out of there immediately. That means, radioactive particles have or are nearby. There aren't going to be many places here that don't have radioactive dust lying about. Just try your best to keep clear, as best you can. Partner up and remember... five minutes only. Any longer than that, you're as good as dead."

Jade looks at Lyle, as he looks back smiling. Lyle grabs the counter as he and Jade make their way out through the triple set of doors. Jade presses the timer on her arm as they breach the last door. The Giger counter goes off immediately, quickly making their way to the waterway that passes by the nuclear plant. The sample bottles clicking and clanking as they make their way down to the inlet. The counter screams, Jade quickly leans down, dipping a specimen cup into the water as Lyle exclaims,

"Jade, two-minute warning!"

Jade gives him a thumbs up, hurriedly dipping in another bottle. Jade, unaware her timer is beeping like mad. Lyle taps her on the shoulder, as she turns to look at him. He points to her arm. Closing up the bottles quickly, they make their way back to the transport. Going through the first of three doors. A thick spray washes over them, followed by a milky substance. A green light comes on, as the second door opens. Jade places the four specimen bottles in a protective case. Closing up the case, placing it in a special drawer. A special set of lights turns on, passing over the duo. Another green light comes on, the door opens as the commander stands before them, and sternly states,

"You two are fourteen seconds late getting back into the transport! Why?"

Jade goes to explain, just as Lyle responds hurriedly,

"Sorry, sir. That was my fault. We were trying to get as many samples as possible. I lost track of seconds."

The commander grimaces as he eyes Lyle, and states irritated,

"Fine! Don't make a habit of this. Otherwise, you'll find out how sick you'll really be. Make sure you two are ready to go again tomorrow at zero eight-hundred. Now, go get some chow in you. Group two should be back soon."

Jade, and Lyle nod as they quickly make their way up to the second floor of this monster transport. Getting back into civilian clothing, Jade, and Lyle sit at a small table. Jade leans over and asks curiously,

"Why did you take the blame for my ignorance?"

Lyle smiles, takes a sip from his metal cup. Placing his cup down, he leans towards Jade and answers softly,

"That's an easy answer any day of the week Jade. You are beautiful and smart. You are in an impossible position, life and death anyway you think of it. Why would I allow anyone to give you an earful for doing your job? If you figured you were in danger, you would have come back. You chose to get that last bottle. There must have been something that told you to get that one…"

Jade interrupts Lyle as she states,

"What if I grabbed it because I lost track of time?"

Lyle laughs as he grabs Jade's hand, and whispers,

"Jade, I met you two days ago. You take what you do seriously, and here is no exception. If I even figured for a second you didn't care, I would not still be by your side. Don't sell yourself short, you knew what you were doing out there."

Jade slowly grins while she looks at Lyle smiling back at her.

Eight A.M. Jade and Lyle ready themselves for another five minutes of frantic collecting. The commander stands in front of them both glaringly, eyeing each of one before responding angrily,

"I don't want another yesterday! Get what you can get in the five minutes that's it. Is that clear?"

Jade and Lyle nod simultaneously, as the commander nods back. Heading back out the series of doors. Running as quickly as the suits allow them to, Jade quickly pulls a bottle out before hitting the edge of the water. Grabbing eight bottles, Lyle taps Jade, as she closes the last bottle up. Making their way through the process of getting back inside the vehicle again.

Six months later. Commander Alex Travois comes running into the dining hall worriedly. Everyone turns towards him as he yells urgently,

"Attention everyone! The Russian's have deduced we are in their hot zone. According to the checklists, most of anything living been collected. We don't have much time left. As I speak, the Russian army is setting up checkpoints along the roads. We are going to head to extraction point Y. Hold on to your drinks, the next few hours are going to be bumpy. Be prepared to abandon anything you can't carry. If the army stops us, we are in for a long few years in their prisons."

The vehicle starts up, the commander grabs onto the nearest doorway as the truck bounces and jerks. Everyone holds onto their tables as the bumps get worst, the faster they go. Unsure where they're going, Jade asks the commander who's lodged himself in the doorway,

"Sir, isn't extraction point Y in the other direction?"

Commander Travois glares at Jade, and responds angrily,

"What do you mean the wrong way? Explain yourself Ms. Mills?"

Jade looks worried, as she answers,

"We passed the Chernobyl plant a few minutes ago. We're headed the way we originally came from six months ago. If that's the case, we're headed straight for the Russian army, sir!"

The commander looks out the side window. He slams his hand against the doorframe enraged, as he stumbles down the stairs headed for the driver. Getting to the driver, he starts yelling,

"Turn around now! We're going the wrong way."

Stinger speeds up, as he yells out,

"Had no choice, sir! While you were gone, they changed extraction point Y, to no extraction point. I'm just trying to get us out of the hot zone, perhaps we can hide in one of the surrounding abandoned cities until they can extract us?"

Commander Travois grimaces as he ponders. Looking at the highway and the hundreds of cars abandoned along the side of the road. He responds sternly,

"Pull over here. I have an idea?"

Stinger pulls the massive transport over to the side of the road. Commander Travois heads back upstairs to the staring eyes of everyone, he states worried,

"New plan! We are going to have to abandon the transport. It appears as if we're NOT being picked up. We are on our own from here on out. We have a few options, one of which is, hiding in the cities that were evacuated months ago. Another, try and get some of these cars up and running again. One thing I will mention now, if you're caught, you're on your own. The government will not back us in any way. I'll leave the choice up to you all to decide. We should be pretty close to the twenty-mile marker. The radiation is still high risk, but lower than by the plant."

Everyone mumbles amongst themselves, as Jade, and Lyle respond,

"If we choose to go on our own, what are the chances of us getting to the border?"

The commander grimaces, as he ponders their question. Soon, he replies,

"Honestly, the nearest border is probably a good fifty miles. Without wheels, and the Russian army heading this way, not well. If you can hide out within the confines of one of the cities, you stand a better chance, but as for the radiation factor, I can't even fathom the thought?"

Jade looks at Lyle concerned, as he answers,

"I believe we stand a better chance leaving the transport. With the size of this vehicle, we stand out like a sore thumb. I know we sent our last specimens out two days ago, so we have no extra baggage to carry with us."

The commander shakes his head annoyed, as he looks around the room. Biting his lip, he states loudly,

"Alright! Jade, Lyle. You two have my permission to go your own ways. The rest of you, choose quickly, as I don't know how far out the Russian army is?"

Jade and Lyle quickly get up and run past the Commander, as he continues talking to the others. Jade looks at Lyle, asking,

"Are you sure about this Lyle?"

Lyle tries to smile, he looks at her kindly, and responds,

"I'm not sure of everything, but the one thing I am sure of. I want you to be free, and to be free, we can't be stuck in here. Now, I will do whatever I have to make that happen. Pack a bag, get your hazmat suit on, and let's fly from this death trap before it's too late."

Jade quickly packs a bag, Lyle comes in holding his. Helping Jade finish packing, as he stuffs some of her items in his bag. They quickly get into their hazmat suits, grab a Giger counter, and head out into the woods near the road.

Two and a half hours later, the echo of machine gun fire crosses Jade and Lyle's ears. They stop, turn around, and then look at each other worried. Lyle grabs Jade's arm, he pulls her along for a second, as she starts running again. The gunfire stops, but the look on Jade's face shows, she knows what happened.

A month after the gunfire, Jade, and Lyle hold up in a hotel, one that has minimal radiation. Trying to determine where they are is hard, as Lyle forgot to grab a compass, or map before they left the transport. Having to hide, as the Russian army passes through the town twice a day. Deciding to follow the army, once the patrol passes through, they follow behind the tank. After following the patrol, they end up near the Russian border. Trying to head through the woods, Jade, and Lyle make their way to a seaport. Buying their way onto a frigate. A week on the sea, Jade, and Lyle talk about continuing the search for marine life. The boat finally hits Alaska. Once on land again, the duo breakdown into tears, knowing they barely made it out of there alive. Jade, decides to call the number they were given at the beginning of this mission in hell. The operator answers,

"Hello… how may I direct your call?"

Jade looks around suspiciously, as a fishing boat blows its horn while she states,

"Five-five-five, five-one-three-three."

The operator pauses, then states,

"Please hold the line, transferring your call now."

The phone begins to ring constantly for a minute before a man answers,

"Hello, is this Jade Mills?"

Jade nods while giving Lyle a weird smile, and answering,

"Yes! How did you know it was me though?"

The man on the phone states urgently,

"Each of you operatives were given a different number to call. Since you called, how many of you made it out of the Chernobyl hot zone alive?"

Jade sighs, as the memories of the gunfire come to the forefront of her mind, tears begin trickling down her cheeks, as she answers,

"I don't know if anyone other than Lyle and myself made it out of there? I know there was gunfire a few hours after we got away from the transport."

The man on the other end sounds disappointed as he replies solemnly,

"Damn… hopefully, they made it out of there. Anyways, since you and Lyle are alive, the money is being transferred to your accounts. You're calling from Nome Alaska. How did you manage to get there?"

Jade looks at Lyle, as she smiles, then answers,

"With the help of Lyle. Without him, I wouldn't be calling you right now."

The man shuffles papers around as if he's looking for something hurriedly. He finally states,

"Good to hear! From what I can see, they have a bank there. Give the teller your name, and if you have that piece of paper, give that to them as well. You should be able to withdraw the money soon, I'll call them right away. I must get going, I'm glad you two made it out alive. One more thing I have to ask before I let you go. Do you want to continue this line of work?"

Jade ponders for a moment, as she remembers what she endured during over the last eight months. As she thinks about it, her mouth shouts out,

"Yes, I do!"

The man gleefully responds,

"Great! I'll send a fax to the bank, contact them, and you'll be part of a larger organization. I'll talk with you again soon Jade. Take some time and relax for a few days. Bye!"

Jade hangs up the phone, turning towards Lyle, and responds unsure,

"I think I signed us up for something else?"

Lyle looks confused, as he tries to form words, but only uttering sounds. Jade continues,

"I don't think it's that bad. I don't think?"

Lyle shakes it off, as he grins, grabbing Jade, hugging her, as he whispers in her ear,

"I'll go anywhere you're going. I love you, Jade."

Jade pulls back a little, as she whispers back,

"I love you too."

They slowly get closer as they begin kissing passionately. A few minutes pass, as Jade, slowly moves back, and replies,

"We better go to the bank. That man said our money is waiting for us there."

Lyle nods, as they walk the half mile to the bank, walking inside, and the lone teller looks at them and nods as she asks while she looks at a paper,

"Are you by chance Jade Mills?"

Jade nods, as she exclaims,

"Yes, I am. Did that man send the money?"

The teller asks,

"Do you have I.D?"

Jade pulls out her piece of I.D, handing it to the lady, as she types something into the computer. She stops for a moment and hands Jade, a piece of paper. Jade grabs the paper from her and looks at it. Turning towards Lyle, and smiles as she responds,

"Do you want to come back to Russia with me again? This time on a research boat?"

Lyle stares at her bewildered, as she passes the paper to him. He glances over it, a smile slowly grows, the more he reads. Finally, he shouts out happily,

"Yes, I'll join you!"

Picking Jade up, and holding her close, they hug, as the teller smiles uncomfortably.

A month and a half later, Jade and Lyle find themselves on a ship, near one of Russia's many rivers that run into the sea. By mid-1988, Jade, and Lyle finally start catching small creatures in their micro nets. Having their own equipment on board helps the process of determining what effects from the Chernobyl meltdown, and which fish have been contained. Spending their days catching microscopic creatures, and their nights embraced in each other's loving arms.

One morning in late October, Lyle calls out excitedly,

"Jade, come here, I found a mutation of sorts?"

Jade quickly runs over, as Lyle puts on a chainmail glove, reaching in and trying to grab something from the plastic pail. Lyle mutters to himself, as he continues to grab for the little dark oddly shaped creature zipping around. Jade watches, laughing, as he concentrates on grabbing this creature. Finally, he shouts,

"Gotcha!"

Putting the pail down, Lyle holds his hand steady, while Jade takes a look at what seems like a squid of some kind? The chainmail starts smoldering, and soon after Lyle begins screaming in pain. Jade tries to take a look, as blood starts to drip on the deck. Lyle screams louder as he shouts,

"Holy shit, it's biting me Jade, and it burns! No, stay back Jade!"

Jade quickly tries to reach for it, to remove it off his hand. Lyle, quickly turns away from her, as he yells,

"NO! Get back Jade!"

Lyle stumbles, as he grabs it with his left hand. Slipping on the pail, he falls over the railing into the sea. She runs for the side screaming,

"LYLE…?"

Looking for any sign of him, as she continues to scream his name. She eventually, falls to her knees on the deck. Looking into the water, tears cascading down her cheeks. Knowing he is gone, taken away by this pint-sized monster. As other members of the crew gather around Jade, she sits there, lost in her own world.

Two weeks after Lyle threw himself off the boat. Jade throws herself into her work, harder than ever. Little does Jade realize, there is another group of people, who are watching her every move? One that may help, or hinder her ability to catch the murderer of her lover?

Jantid

1989

Admiral Mundane, sits in the briefing cabin next to his quarters, watching as his intelligence officer paces back and forth, holding papers while glancing up occasionally, as he states,

"Since early 1989, the shipping lanes in South America, specifically in the South Pacific Ocean have been plagued with ships vanishing. Authorities puzzled by these new events... No hurricanes or typhoons at the times of the S.O.S beacons being sent out. In almost every case, there is no debris floating around. Conspiracy theorists have offered many alternative answers, but no facts to back them up. The U.S and Mexican Governments have united, in a joint effort to find out why? After almost a year of exploring the waters, where all the transmissions came from, they have discovered little bits of wreckage from the last ship that disappeared...the Squirmy rose, a sixty-three-foot yacht with a family of eight aboard. Presuming the other wreckages were swept away by the currents, they have closed the books with the Ministers involved stating, these are random accidents and nothing more. What should we do Admiral?"

Glaring at the intelligence officer, cupping his hands while answering sternly,

"If they have concluded their findings, we must abide with those findings as well."

Months go by before another ship sends a distress signal from that area, this time a partially recorded message by the coast guard who are in route to the Freighter Alvin's Quest, This is that message;

"Mayday, mayday…this is the Alvin's Quest… (Static) …we…something big! …holes in bulkheads one, three, and five! Can anyone hear us? I have sent the distress signal out…over…Dear God, what is that white stuff... (Static) then dead."

When the Coast guard Ship Tampa arrives twenty-seven minutes later, they find a man barely alive and pull him aboard. Gerald Salome, the man pulled from the ocean answers fearfully,

"Thank you, thank you! You saved my life… Oh my God! Huge… monster…! Tentacles, an octopus, or squid…?"

The man dies shortly after. After searching the area and finding nothing more, they head home. A bleep showing something about sixty-eight feet long and then disappears, the crew assumes it is a piece of the ship sinking to the bottom and continue home. During the way, the doctor heads to the Admirals quarters to discuss what the man said to him. (Knocking on the door) The two sit down and try to decipher what Gerald Salome meant by his last words. The doctor states,

"His exact words were… huge monster, octopus, or squid!"
Admiral Mundane looks at Doctor Simons with a raised brow before answering,

"Why on God's green earth, would octopuses, and squids be attacking ships for anyways?"

Dr. Simons shakes his head, not sure himself as he responds,

"Perhaps it was something he had encountered before?"

Admiral Mundane leans forward, looking Dr. Simon in the eyes hard, and replies,

"And perhaps it is an Oldman's riddle that has no meaning… being as that object we saw was approximately 70 feet long, it may have been a whale that hit their boat! I think we can just chalk this down to an accident!"

Looking into the cold hard stare of the Admiral, Dr. Simon just nods his head in agreement.

July 4th long weekend 1996

Cancun Mexico; People wandering the beach enjoying the summer's suns torment, while others splash in the waters cool soothing embrace. A couple out in the water on a yellow sailboat, enjoying the breeze taking them further out. A slim young waiter in his early twenties, delivering drinks to a group of women sitting in the shade giggling playfully. A peaceful serenity, only broken by the excessive ranting of a bulky man who seems to want everyone to hear what he has to say. Another older well-dressed waiter comes walking towards the bulky man's table angrily, and announces loudly while everyone on the patio turns quickly shocked by what they hear,

"Excuse me, sir…can you shut up for a while?"

Turning shocked by the waiter's loud message, glaring up towards the waiter, as he arrogantly answers while sitting up straight,

"Who the hell are you to tell me what to do? You do not own this place, do you…?"

The waiter grimaces at the man, and pleasantly responds knowing the man is irate and ready to explode,

"No, I do not sir, some of our guests come here to enjoy the peace and 'quiet!' Which your loud bolstering voice seems to be abrasive to their peaceful serenity."

The burly man slams the table with his right hand as he shouts out,

"Well EXCUSE me Mister BOSS, I am here to enjoy myself too! Why do you not just be as a migrating bird and FLOCK off?"

The burly man balls his fists up, as anger pours out of his glaring eyes. The waiter grips the tray tighter, and the look on his face changes, slightly more defensive, while he slowly makes a fist as he replies semi-calm.

"Why don't…."

Another man dressed in a suit with a manager tag comes running over. Exclaiming, as the waiter turns to look, while the bulky man stands up,

"Excuse me, gentlemen…you both are disturbing our guests. Let's go elsewhere and discuss this matter."

The waiter nods at the manager, and responds cheerfully,

"Oh, I am sorry, I said my peace. You have a good day sir."
The burly man flaps his hands in a bird flying motion while stating loudly, as the waiter walks away,
"That is right boy, at least you know when to leave little birdy!"

The disgruntled man smiling as the manager pushes the disgruntled man back down in his chair, as he tries to go walking after the waiter. He leans towards the burly man, and angrily responds,

"Quickly drink up sir. You will have to leave the hotel, hurry up, and come with me, sir."

The man glares up at the manager's angry stare, and chugs his drink back, placing the glass down hard. The suited man grabs the disgruntled man's arm and leads the man towards the exit. Minutes later, as people turn back, and enjoy the peace once again. An elderly man walking along the shoreline as waves run across his feet lightly comes to a stop. Cupping his hands over his eyes, as he strains to see what the shadow in a coming wave is? Staring even harder at the object that's seemingly growing in size, a shocked expression takes hold of his face as he yells while pointing,

"SHARK! SHARK!"

People hurriedly stand up and look out into the surf where the man is pointing. A twelve-foot Great white shark is heading right for the beach at top speed. People scream in horror, then confusion, as the shark swims by the people in the water, and beaches itself. Soon, the sharks followed by other large fish beaching themselves, some barely in a foot of water. Swimmers make their way back to shore in amongst the thousands of fish zooming past them, everyone begins making his or her way to the water's edge to watch this once-in-a-lifetime spectacle. As swimmers step on fish, they slip and fall as they scurry their way back onto the beach. Terrified as they look back at the water. Lifeguards run over to bewildered swimmers who are making their way over the building wall of flailing fish. One tall lifeguard shouts confused,

"What the hell is going on out in the surf?"

Holding onto one man's arm, as he helps him over the continuing fish swarm, his arm bleeding profusely, as he responds dazed,

Jantid

"I, I didn't see anything, except thousands of fish that came swimming by, one grazed my arm cutting it open…I thought I was a dead man when I saw that shark coming…he just swam by me like I was not there. I tried looking behind me, but it was so murky with fish, I could not see anything, I swam until I hit shore. I just knew whatever had that shark scared enough to bolt past me like that, had to be something I didn't want to meet?"

The swimmer looks petrified looking at the shark flailing around not more than fifteen feet away. The lifeguard wraps the man's arm up as he continues to stare at the shark, shaking his head in disbelief. He nudges the man back to reality. Helping the man to his feet again as he replies,

"Okay, come with me, we will get that gash taken care of."

As more people help the other swimmers get past the wall of fish that are still accumulating on or near the shore. People's screams of fear can be heard hundreds of yards away as the chaos continues to unfold. Everyone focuses on getting all the swimmers out of the water, as a yellow sailboat continues its trek a couple of miles away from shore.

An older couple sit near the stern of their boat, watching where they're headed. Richard leans towards Jenny grinning, and whispers playfully,

"I am so glad we came here this year Jenny…so picturesque!"

She smiles gleefully, and looks out towards the open water smiling, as Jenny answers,

"Oh yes, we could stay out here forever Richard… hey? Look at those fish?"

As Richard leans forward, and stares at the water, confused by their erratic swimming, shooting past their boat heading towards shore. Richard replies puzzled,

"Wow, they are really moving, must be a shark close by? They are spooked something fierce headed towards the shore. Jenny, hand me the binoculars?"

Richard quickly snaps a few pictures of the fish. Turning the other way, trying to catch a picture of this shark. Jenny responds annoyed,

"I will shortly, I just want to enjoy this view."

Richard, not seeing anything, turns the camera towards shore and looks as something nudges their boat, causing it to sway, as he responds worriedly,

"Okay, but looks as if there's a commotion on shore, look for yourself!"

Putting her hands over her eyes blocking the glare of the sun on the water, Jenny looks, and then turns to Richard and asks nervously,

"I wonder what is happening on shore?"

Richard gives an annoyed expression towards Jenny, as he shouts,

"That is why I want the binoculars, jeez!"

Jenny hurriedly digs through the drawer, and angrily slams him in the stomach with them and replies angrily,

"Fine, here they are…"

26

Grabbing the binoculars, giving Jenny a dirty look, as he puts them to his eyes, and shockingly responds a few seconds later,

"Holy cow! There is a couple of sharks that look beached…looks like everyone is watching them. Ha-ha!"

Richard lowers the binoculars, as he laughs harder, Jenny starts laughing, as she states loudly,

"I say let those sharks die…they are not useful for anything anyway."

Richard stops laughing long enough to spurt out,

"They are Jenny, they are great in soup. Ha-ha!"

Jenny gasps from laughing so hard, as she takes a couple of deep breaths and responds,

"Oh, Richard…! Wait? What is that? That is an awful big shadow in the water below us."

As they both look over the side, as an immense dark shadow just under the surface that continues to grow. Richard and Jenny look at each other fearfully, as Richard responds,

"Yeah, that has to be three times the size of our boat, that thing has to be at least eighty feet long? Whatever it is, it is underneath us…just keep calm…perhaps it will pass?"

Jenny goes back to watching the shadow, as he begins turning the boat towards the beach. Jenny looks at Richard, fear overwhelming her, as she whispers,

"What is it?"

Richard looks back at the water, as he replies just as scared,

"I do not know what that is? I don't recognize the shape? Maybe it's a school of something?"

Jenny has tears in her eyes, as she shakenly whimpers,

"I am worried Richard, let's head back!"

Richard still watches, as the mass seems to have no end. He nods slowly, as he responds,

"I'm doing what I can, we will head back, as soon as I swing the sail around, hang on…"

Jenny gets a strange fearful look on her face, as the mass gets darker. Tapping Richard on the shoulder, as she quietly replies,

"Richard that shadow looks like it's getting bigger, look!"

Richards's eyes bulge, as he watches this huge mass become more clear, covering his mouth as he responds quietly,

"Oh my God! Come on move faster! WHAT THE HELL IS THAT?"

As he tries to get the sail positioned right, anxiously attempting to catch the breeze, Jenny screams,

"OH 'God' we are going to die!"

At that same moment, the sailboats hit hard from underneath sending Jenny, and Richard splashing into the water screaming. Watching in horror as their boat starts to get pulled under, a tentacle comes up quickly. Flopping itself across the deck. Pulling it under the surface in one big explosion of water and fiberglass. Richard and

28

Jenny watch their yellow sails grabbed by what could only be described as huge deformed tentacles.

Frantically, they both swim towards the shore, Jenny swims into a white patch floating at the surface, and stops swimming, as a look of pain, and fear comes over her face. Richard stops swimming, as he watches his love, Jenny slowly disappear into the white stringy things attached to her face as she tries to move. Richard looks underwater and is horrified, as he watches Jenny being carried down to the depths. Turning his head underneath himself as he sees the huge inside of a beak break the surface, turning around, and seeing the other side behind him. Richard screams,

"GOD NO…!"

As he begins swimming trying to get away from the closing beak, only to have it snap shut. The shadow of the creature slowly returns to the murkiness of the deep.

#2

Dawn approaches on the horizon, Juan, and Damian from the resort hotel head to the beach to clean up any mess left behind from yesterday's unexplainable beaching of thousands of fish. Shining flashlights along their way. (Splash) Turning to look where this deafening sound came from, the water recedes at good ten-feet, before coming back hitting their feet. Damien shines his light out on the water cautiously, as he responds frightened,

"What the heck was that Juan?"

Juan who nervously scans the water with his light. Stopping when he sees water rippling near the shore, and replies nervously,

"I do not know, but let us make our way quickly, I do not want to be this close to the water. Not after what happened yesterday."

Damien nods anxiously, as his eyes make their way from right to left in an attempt to catch anything other than the water moving. Whispering back,

"Yeah, me neither, anything that can move that much water cannot be good. Juan? … Juan… Hey, where are you? Quit messing around, JUAN, come on?"

(Splash) a small muffled sound. Turning around shining the flashlight hurriedly towards the noise. Running to where Juan was just standing, looking at Juan's hat laying on the sand while the nearby water is rippling like someone just threw a big rock. Damien calls out loudly,

"Come on Juan, your hats in the water, quit messing around, or I will tell Mr. Bell. Juan, hey man, come on. Fine, you stay here, I am going back to the hotel."

Feeling this overwhelming need to run, Damien bolts back to the hotel, hearing a clicking sound, turning and seeing nothing, stumbling and falling onto the sand. Seeing a shadow moving above the water then disappear. Rubbing his eyes profusely trying to focus. Mr. Bell stands just in front of him, and yells,

"Damen! Why you lying on the beach, you and Juan are supposed to be picking up garbage. I suppose Juan is laying around as well?"

Staring back out onto the water, Damien fearfully answers,

"No sir, Mr. Bell, we were cleaning up, we heard a loud splash, and then Juan was gone."

Mr. Bell glares down at Damien with disgust, as he replies angrily,

"Oh come on, you could not come up with something better than that. You know the Marlins are probably hunting food right now. I've had enough of this Damien, turn in your uniform, you and Juan are fired! When you see him, tell him to come see me right away. Now go!"

While Damen runs into the hotel, Mr. Bell looks out at the ocean, the sun beginning to creep up in the sky. Walking towards the beach in the orange sky that begins reflecting on the water's surface. Looking at something in the distance, about three hundred yards out. Then a quick splash and gone. Shaking his head in disbelief, he continues to walk down the beach looking to see how much garbage is left lying around. After a short while coming across Juan's hat floating a couple of feet out in the surf. Looking around to see where Juan is…nowhere around. Hearing a man panting as he stops, as Mr. Bell turns and sees Mr. O'Brien, his assistant standing there, pointing towards the pier and responds gasping,

"Excuse me Mr. Bell. We have a problem down at the pier sir."

As they look towards the pier, Mr. Bell asks confused,

"Well? What is it Mr. O'Brien?"

Looking at each other as Mr. O'Brien looks worried, as he replies,

"To put it straight, someone vandalized four boats last night."

Mr. Bell gets an angry expression on his face, as he answers irritably,

"How did someone get onto that pier? Was it not locked up yesterday at eleven?"

Nodding, Mr. O'Brien replies,

"It was sir! Seems they would have come by boat, I also know there are two that are damaged badly."

Mr. Bell runs his hand over his face trying to stay calm as he responds questioningly,

"How do you know this?"

Mr. O'Brien looks towards the pier as he answers,

"Well, first the police should be here in a while, but there is an arm floating by the dock, I think one of them got cocky and crushed his arm between a boat and the bumper. Not really floating, but caught on the bumper in the water."

Mr. Bell glares as he responds agitatedly,

"Well make sure you tell the police that!"

Mr. O'Brien nods, as he turns slightly, hearing sirens, he responds quickly,

"I will sir, I better get back to the pier, I hear what sounds like the police coming."

Waving his hand agitatedly towards Mr. O'Brien, as he starts running down the beach until he gets to the pier a couple miles down. Getting to the Pier just in time to watch a police officer fishing the arm out of the water, and placing it in a bag, the police officers walk around and survey the damage to the boats. Finding two of the boats structures damage too extensive stay in the water. An officer walks over to the night watchman, as he cringes for a moment. The officer seems to see this, stopping in front of Mr. Wylda. He glares at him as he asks,

"So what can you tell me, about what happened here?"

Mr. Wylda looks frightened, he tries adjusting his posture, and replies,

"I do not really know…I fell asleep, I woke up when I heard the boats hit the dock. There was nothing out there, except the boats rocking back and forth."

The officer glares, as he scans the surroundings while he questioningly asks,

"Were there any people around at all… anyone that may have seen something going on?"

Mr. Wylda shakes his head, as he points to the damaged boats and answers,

"No officer, just the boats, and a loud splash, nothing a man could make, I assumed maybe a seal or sea lion. They sometimes stop and sit on the rocks over there for a while."

The officer writes down the information, as he asks suspiciously,

"I see, there was an arm found right down there by the edge of this pier, are you 'sure' there was no people around? These sea lions, have you seen any around lately?"

Mr. Wylda's eye widen, as he gulps and replies,

"Yes, I am sure. After I heard the boat hit the dock, I turned all the spotlights on and nobody was out there. Come to think of it, I haven't seen any sea lions in a few weeks?"

The officer continues to write as he occasionally glances up with a hard look. He closes up his notepad as he responds,

"Interesting, I may come back and talk with you some more?"

Mr. Wylda stares at the officer concerned, as he replies,

"Yes, of course, I will be inside my office."

The officer glances over at Mr. Wylda, almost scurrying away. Scanning the walkways, trying to get a hold of what happened here last night, before heading back to the dock, where another Detective comes walking over. As he points towards the dock bumper with his pen and replies confidently,

"The arm was not removed here. There is no trace of blood splatter anywhere on this dock."

The officer looks back at Mr. Wylda's office, and responds even more suspiciously,

"Okay, I'll take this evidence to the lab, perhaps we can find out who this arm belongs too?"

The detective shakes his head in disbelief, as he looks towards the damaged boat, and replies frustrated,

"Yes, I will leave this case up to you to handle for now, when the evidence is processed, I'll return to this case. I'll be going back to my other ongoing case. If you find out who, or what happened here before the evidence comes back, call me!"

The officer nods agreeing while gazing at the bumper bewildered as he responds irritated,

"I will. Thanks' for coming out anyways."

The detective walks over to the damage, and points out the damage on the bumper compared to the boat and responds knowingly,

"No problem, truthfully, I would suspect just by the way these boats were hit, it was probably another boat that hit them."

The officer nods agreeing, as he watches the detective while answering irritated,

"That is what I was starting to think myself, but now we must find that boat."

The detective looks at his watch and replies impatiently,

"I will leave you to it to figure out officer…"

Walking away, the officer goes back to looking around for any clues. The detective's radio crackles to life,

"We found a dead shark four miles up the coastline…something tore it up extremely well."

Grabbing the radio while walking to his car, the detective answers curiously,

"Do you know what bit the shark… over?"

The woman on the other end responds,

"Negative, but it only has a head to where the gills start, I think?"

The detective shakes his head again, as he replies annoyed,

"Alright, I'll make my way over there…over."

The woman answers,

"Okay, see you when you get here…over, and out!"

As the detective drives down the road, he slams on the brakes, quickly pulling over to the side of the road. Flinging his door open, he runs across the road heading to the beach. Making his way down the embankment. Through the waist-high bushes onto the beach, looking into the water and slowly making his way closer. Cupping his hands above his eyes to block the sun's rays, trying to figure if the sun is playing with his eyes, or if there is something in the water. Grabbing his radio, He states sternly,

"Carlo's, you in the air?"

Carlo responds a minute later,

"No, just at the airport refueling. What do you need Frank?"

Still staring out onto the water intently, the detective responds,

"Could you fly over a section of ocean, about five miles east of the Cancun resort?"

Carlo doesn't reply right away, watching what looks like something massive floating. Carlo finally answers,

"Roger! Give me ten minutes. What am I looking for? Over."

The detective continues to look at the mass, as he answers,

"Thanks' I cannot say exactly, it looks like it is approximately about one-one hundred and fifty yards out. Over."

Carlo replies as the sound of the helicopter's engine firing up interrupts his answering,

"Roger, I am taking off now. I will be at your location in about four minutes. Over."

The detective still watches, as he replies hoping,

"Roger, I will stay here until you arrive. Over."

Watching as the mass begins to slowly fade into the water. Five minutes pass before the helicopter is overhead flying around. Grabbing his radio asking,

"Can you see anything Carlos, over?"

Carlos takes a couple of circular passes as he does these, taking a look out the door, he stares down into the water for a moment, then responds amused,

"Yes Frank, a dead whale shark. I will try to position myself over it, and you can tell me if that is where you saw it. Over."

The Frank watches as the helicopter swings down maybe ten-feet above the water. He responds confidently,

"Roger. That looks about right. Over."

Carlos clicks the radio twice, and pauses, as his helicopter sways over to the side, and he responds clearly,

"Other than that, there is a huge school of fish bigger than the whale shark carcass below it. Wait a minute…?"

The helicopter gets even closer to the water as detective Frank asks curiously,

"What is it, Carlos? Carlos…?"

Looking at the helicopter do a quick round-about as he replies uncertain,

"Hang on a moment, Frank? I am going to try to get lower and see, it's not moving like any school of fish that I've ever seen before?"

The helicopter's altitude drops until it's close to the water's surface spraying water all around. Frank can barely make out the helicopter in the spray, as he responds worried,

"What is going on Carlos?"

Carlos replies as the helicopter reveals the carcass in the spray. Carlos answers perplexed,

"I am going to try and hook the carcass and bring it in. I want to see if whatever is underneath the whale shark is going to follow me in. Over."

Frank gives a thumbs up while worrying that Carlos is way too close to the water. Taking a deep breath before replying,

"Roger, let me know when you have it, and please be careful. Over."

Watching with hands blocking the sun, seeing another man dropping what might be a rope into the water after the helicopter lifts up a couple of times, the radio cracks to life as Carlos replies confidently,

"I have it hooked, bringing it in now."

The helicopter's engine powers up, and begins coming towards the shore slowly. Watching as the helicopter tilts to the right and does a half circle. Carlos replies a little fearful,

"Holy shit! You had better move back Frank, by the weight of what I am pulling, whatever that thing or things are, they are attached to this whale shark carcass. I'm at full power and it's still fighting me hard."

Watching at the helicopter bouncing around erratically, as the Detective responds concerned,

"Carlos, can you see what it is that's got ahold of the carcass?"

Listening as the engine sounds like its maxing out its horsepower. Frank watches fearfully, as the helicopter zigs-zags back and forth hard, as Carlo replies,

"Negative, but it is a powerhouse, whatever it is? I have barely moved forward twenty-feet."

Just as he finishes saying that the whale shark carcass flies out of the water sending it into the bottom of the helicopter. Both the carcass and the helicopter hit the water, watching in horror as it bursts into flames and begins to sink. A nearby boat races over trying to help. The radio cracks to life as Frank stands there, open-mouthed trying to comprehend what he just saw.

"Hello? Hello? If you can hear us, officer, we are aboard the boat, Yana's dream, we will try and get that man or men from the water."

Seeing the boat come speeding towards the smoke and debris as the Detective responds,

"Thank you, folks. I will wait to hear from you again."

Aboard the boat, using a gaff to reach into the water. Grabbing bits and pieces out of the water, as Dale points to something about ten-feet below the surface, and replies curiously,

"Hey, Tim, what in the Dicken's is that thing?"

Tim leans over and looks, as he replies puzzled,

"Geez, I am not sure, looks messed up, maybe from when the helicopter came splashing down?"

Dale tries to catch it with the gaff, as it moves to the side, and down just out of reach. As he keeps trying to catch it, Dale responds while a lifejacket pops up to the surface,

"Yeah, could be, it's huge whatever that is. Get the net and grab those pieces floating right there. Good, you got it. I guess he must have drowned in the helicopter. Let's head in and give the officer what we have."

Putting the lifejacket down with the other items, as Tim looks towards the silhouette of Frank on the shore. Tim looks in the water, and shouts scared,

"Holy shit Dale… it's gone?"

Dale looks over the side, and responds cautiously while looking around,

"What the heck…? Where'd it go?"

Tim looks over the side, as the boat heads towards the shoreline. Seeing what looks like the edge of a tentacle as the boat zips passed.

#3

Sitting at his desk frustrated, Detective Frank Jordan goes over the after pictures of the helicopter crash. Not having recovered either Carlo, Andrews, or the helicopter wreckage, shaking his head, as he tries to piece this whole thing together into one piece. Remembering about the whale shark carcass that wasn't found either? Grabbing another folder and looking at the shark head that was devoured by something larger than a presumed twenty-foot shark. Placing the picture beside the pictures of the debris found by the boaters. The phone rings, as Detective Jordan answers frustrated,

"Hello!"

The lady on the other side responds,

"Hello, is Frank Jorden there?"

Rubbing his face, as he tries to calmly answer,

"Yes, I am Frank Jordan, what can I do for you?"

The woman sounds happier, as she responds,

Jantid

"Great, I am calling from Robert's DNA lab and coding. We received a sample tissue of unknown origin from your department last week."

Frank sits forward anticipating good news, as he answers quickly,

"Yes, we sent that a week ago, do you have the results?"

The woman hesitates momentarily, then replies reserved,

"Yes and no, what you sent us is either really decomposed, or it is a species of animal that has not been around in millions of years…?"

Shocked. Trying to get his head around this, Frank takes a breath, and responds bewildered,

"…What do you mean, when I sent that sample, it was fresh off of whatever that tissue came from."

The lady pauses momentarily as papers shuffle. She responds excitedly,

"Really, well if that is the case, you may have discovered a new species. The DNA comes back to a few different species…the rest is of an unknown origin. The one animal is squid, and the other is stingray, the forty-three percent is unknown. So, unless your samples contaminated…that is your answer Mr. Jorden. I'm sorry I can't be more helpful."

Staring at the shark head, as Frank ponders this new information. Grabbing the photo, and asking,

"Really, squid and stingray? How big might something like that be, I mean how big could something like that grow to?"

The woman responds cautiously,

"I honestly do not know, I guess that may depend on what parts of the DNA strands each one is carrying? Like a puzzle, each piece has to fit nicely into another piece. If it does not fit, there is a possibility of a mutation, but something living like that would almost surely render it useless or it would die shortly after birth. For each individual, a ray could grow in excess of ten feet. The squid, perhaps anywhere from three to seventy-feet. This is just me speculating detective, I can't give you a specific species. This answer would be different if I had more to compare it to, but I don't."

Placing the photo of the shark head down, leaning back Frank responds urgently,

"I am sorry to ask so many questions, but we have had a few incidents here involving something unknown to us. If you can tell me anything else…?"

The woman shuffles more papers, as she responds empathetically,

"No, I understand, if you like, we have a field worker working near Mexico. Might take her a day to reach you. I can easily have everything we found delivered overnight if you prefer Detective?"

Frank smiles, as he nods and replies relieved,

"Yes, thank you. I would be grateful, we all want to find out what this creature is."

The lady sounds delighted as she answers,

"Okay, I will send a message to Jade Mills, and send all these reports back to your office…same address?"

Frank responds as he jots down her name,

"Yes…Jade Mills is her name?"

The woman responds quickly,

"Yes, I will tell her to meet you when she docks. I must go if I am going to send this out today. Bye Mr. Jorden."

Frank smiles as he answers,

"Bye!"

Hanging up, the phone Janice, looking over at Frank, and comes walking towards him and asks curiously,

"What's up, Frank?"

Frank looks up at her, and grabs the shark photo, and asks,

"Janice, what do you know about marine biology?"

Janice looks confused, as she responds suspiciously,

"I know a little bit, not enough to make a dollar though. Why?"

Frank continues to smile as he hands Janice the photo, and responds,

"That place that called, we sent that tissue sample those boaters pulled out of the water after Carlos helicopter crashed. The woman on the phone said this thing is part squid, ray and something unknown. I am wondering if our samples have been cross-contaminated. Or is it possible we have a creature that is actually all these things…and more?"

Janice grimaces, as she answers unsure,

"Huh? Okay, I know what you are saying; I guess it may be possible that species cross-breed, but that would be a hundred thousand to one. I handled those samples myself, the only way any squid or ray would be in them, is if they were already in there. You know…let me check the files here."

Frank sits forward again, as Janice walks over to a nearby filing cabinet. Frank asks,

"What are you looking for exactly?"

Janice grabs a folder out, and starts flipping through it and replies,

"We were sent something a while back…here it is…yes, this is it. This is from both the Mexican and U.S. Governments, regarding ships that have gone missing over the past seven years. That is two-hundred miles from us. What if the disappearance of Richard and Jenny Whiner, is because of what happened to these boats?"

Frank clasps his hands together, as he looks intrigued and skeptical as he responds,

"Let me get this right? You think that what happened to fifty thousand plus ton ships has moved here, to our shores?"

Janice nods, as she passes the notification to Frank, as she continues to explain,

"Yes, that would explain enough of these occurrences that have happened in the past couple of weeks. How else do you explain practically every fish in probably a hundred-mile plus radius ending up on our beach?"

Frank shakes his head puzzled, as he reads the notification, and then responds doubtfully,

"This cannot be the same thing that would mean it's coming to shallow waters and making itself seen. They say it is about eighty plus feet long! This one is only about sixty feet. If those boaters are right in what they said?"

Janice replies sternly,

"Yes, remember though, these are approximations, not accurate measurements. Since those ships have orders to reroute north to avoid the sinking of ships in this area. Perhaps this creature has migrated to our shores for food instead of following those ships."

Frank continues to ponder, as he glances at the photos spew on his desk. Stopping and nodding as he loudly exclaims,

"That is right too, they moved the shipping lines months ago. You are a genius, Janice! Soon you will have my job (Ha-ha!) I cannot believe it. Now we just have to figure out what it is, and a way to kill it?"

Janice smiles, as she leans down and looks at the pictures of the little bits of helicopter wreckage, and responds,

"We know this thing does not have many predators to fend off. We know it is big, probably too big for any nets we have. We also know it stays near the bottom. There is no way the government will let us close the beach until this thing moves on."

Frank nods agreeing, as he shifts his eyes towards Janice and answers,

"Yes, all true, perhaps we can get pictures of it? At least have some possibility of getting a clear picture of it…before I forget, there is a woman coming down, her name is Jade Mills, since you have more expertise than anyone else does here, you, and Jade figure this out. I will go and try to get us some support to deal with this situation."

Janice looks shocked, and excited, as she replies,

"Yes, I will do my best to help this woman Jade in any way I can."

Frank smiles, as he answers,

"I know you will Janice."

Jantid

#4

The next morning, a seventy-foot ship begins descending on the shores, only fifty-feet out. Heading towards the outer docks. Janice goes to greet Jade, who radioed in before making her approach. Getting there just as she is tying the last rope down, Jade looks up smiling, her light brown hair in two ponytails hanging down the front of her chest. Janice smiles, as she holds her hand out and responds excitedly,

"Hi, you must be Jade?"

Jade smiles, as she grasps her hand, and responds happily,

"Hi, yes I am. Jade Mills! You must be officer…?"

Janice nervously smiles, as she replies,

"Yes, sorry, Janice Tore's. I have been so busy lately, last night we had three people go missing and on and on."

Jade nods concerned, as she asks inquisitively,

"Do you think it's this mutation that caused these three people to go missing?"

Janice looks puzzled, as she responds,

"Mutation? I thought a mutant would not survive?"

Jade watches, as a couple of men pass by, and then replies quietly,

"Most do not make it past a day… do you have a private spot where we can talk?"

Janice watches, as the men stop within listening distance, as she nods, and replies,

"Oh yes of course, right this way."

Walking back to the office, as the two men in suits try to follow behind. They turn and walk away once Jade, and Janice make their way into the police station. Grabbing two cups of coffee and sitting down. Jade pulls papers and files out of a briefcase. Janice grabs the package that arrived earlier. Jade looks Janice in the eyes, and whispers,

"Okay, everything said here must remain between us ONLY! This research is of the highest security. Do you understand Janice?"

Janice looks worried, as she whispers back,

"Yes, yes I understand!"

Jade opens a file, and passes Janice a page, as she responds quickly,

Jantid

"A day after the Chernobyl reactor failed, the U.S. sent in stealth troopers. These were biochemists, biologists among others. They collected samples of everything living, under the program, (World destruction) they brought everything from the 'hot zone' where the radiation was at the most critical. Everything extracted, including the Stealth troopers who all died, to an underground facility. For the next five years, everything monitored every second of every day. Here are some of what they found. See in this photo, on one side you see the normal microbes, on the other side, you'll see the mutations from Chernobyl. This whole pile right here is the same, various changes in the molecular structure of each one of these living animals, bugs right up to the human beings, everything just from the hot zone."

Janice saddened look says it all, as she replies sorrowfully,

"Dear God, so different from one side to the next…radiation did this to all these animals, humans, and what not?"

Jade nods, as she pulls more pages out, and answers,

"Yes, everything on the right side is mutated, the biggest changes are seen in the smaller ones, some of the pictures, especially the smaller microbes are hours apart. The bigger animals and fish are months to years apart. Depending on the levels of radiation, some of the larger animals showed even quicker mutations, same with the smaller ones too."

Janice shakes her head slowly, as she responds,

"So what, did they send people in to get the animals out?"

Jade shakes her head no, as she looks around, and replies in a whisper,

"No, once Russian officials realized what was happening, they decided to seal off an access. Setting up checkpoints, no one's allowed past certain points. Therefore, everything is alive, even after many warning about what may be stewing inside their waterways. We showed them everything we had, but all involved have rejected them. We monitor what we can, and sometimes catch a new species, others slip by."

Janice looks horrified, as she answers just as quiet,

"They just ignored what you found?"

Jade takes a sip of her coffee, and responds as she hands Janice another piece of paper,

"Not what I found, I have been working three years in this general area, trying to catch or kill this monstrosity. The problem I have is, this creature is translucent until it is ready to strike. I know they do not want anyone knowing what species it is, but I feel I must tell you. We know all the animals that make it up…squid, something from the stingray family, and jellyfish of some kind."

Janice looks at the paper almost speechless, as she stares at Jade and replies,

"I know Frank, the detective in charge said he was told about the squid and stingray. Jellyfish. Seems like a strange combination?"

Jade looks around the room, as she replies,

"Yes, from what we can figure out, and this is just a theory. I personally figure, either it started as a one cell microbe of any one of these animals…somehow, it moved through the rivers, or across the land. Possibly making its way to the ocean. Keep in mind, these things would still be mutating. So either it ate or was eaten by another

52

fish and began transforming and slowly became what we have here today? I have no real proof, just a thousand theories. The only thing I can say with any amount of certainty is the squid is the largest amount of DNA."

Janice nods, as she answers concerned,

"Yeah, I guess it would be hard to figure the origins if you do not have the evidence. I know it is wreaking havoc here."

Jade glances at Janice while pulling a picture out of the folder, and responding,

"Yes, that is why I am being so open with you Janice…three years I have been hunting it, waiting for an opting moment, this is that moment. This thing is in shallow enough water now that we can track movements, unlike when it was in deep water, I could not do anything but hope I was going the right way."

Janice looks at the picture, as she replies,

"Is this it… so small? I am behind you every step of the way Jade! What do we all need, I will try and round it up?"

Jade nods, as she replies,

"I believe I have everything needed aboard my boat. I had better warn you of another thing I know as well. There is a reason no other ships, are ever recovered, it seems to corrode all metals upon contact. When I first began searching, my assistant and I caught something in a net, this thing was maybe six inches long, looked like a messed up glob of goo. Lyle, my assistant, put chainmail gloves on, to grab this thing. He picks it up, and just, as he is ready to place it, so I can take a picture…a smell of sulfuric acid and his gloves start melting. I guess the pain must have been bad, he ended up jumping into the water…never saw him again. I cannot say, but I believe, just a little bit, that this is the same creature."

Janice looks mortified, as she stares at the badly taken picture, and replies,

"Oh wow! That would explain the damage to those boats, that thing must have swum through the harbor, close to where you are docked now."

Janice hands the picture back, as Jade responds,

"Yeah, I made sure mine is made of non-metal outer pieces, will not stop it from dragging the boat down, but at least it will not disappear into the unknown. Perhaps we can set water camera's up, and try and locate this mutant."

Janice hands back the rest of the papers, and responds,

"Yes, I guess if you want to hit the water, we should take your boat."

Jade smiles, and responds smiling,

"Good idea!"

#5

Mr. Frank Jorden sits in front of a committee of six men and four women trying to get help with removing this mysterious monster that has taken refuge along the shores of Cancun. Mr. Jack Froze grimaces harshly before speaking up after listening to Mr. Jorden's pleas.

"Look, I understand your position Mr. Jorden…sending an army to Cancun would not be the best course of action at this moment in time. What do you think the tourists will do? Leave. If they see a building military presence… that is what they will do… leave. I'm sorry, I just can't cause this burden to fall on the businesses that count on the tourists that visit here… "

Mr. Jordan, shakes his head frustrated while he stands up, and replies loudly,

"Mr. Froze! Let's say your family was there in Cancun, I mean right now. Your kids go missing with no trace, then what. Are you still going to think that same way? No! You will search to no ends to find them. Three teens went missing last night. Three people are just a few in an entire mess of missing people, damaged boats, and even lost ones. This thing, or whatever it is—is going to stay here until the only living things here is that monster. I cannot stand by as you do nothing,

I had hoped you all would understand the plight we are facing right now. "

Mr. Froze grimaces at Mr. Jorden with distaste as he states irritated,

"Okay Mr. Jorden, I get it alright. We will send an investigator out and see if your pleas warrant such actions. First though, I want to know about these teens you mentioned? What exactly happened to them?"

Mr. Jordan sits down, opens a folder, spending a moment glancing over the paper while answering,

"Yes, Sir! According to Ms. Tore's, two young women, and a man went down to the beach to enjoy an evening fire at the pits. We allow them there, I guess a few others went to join them. When they got there, nobody was around. They found some drag marks, looking like all three teens were dragged into the ocean. The officer there took pictures of the scene before the tides could wash them away. May I approach to show them to you?"

Mr. Froze nods and responds slightly warmer,

"Yes, please do."

Mr. Jordan stands up, and walks to each member, and passes the pictures to each person while responding worriedly,

"Thank you. See here, that is blood along the side of the drag marks. Something grabbed these kids, and no one knows exactly what is going on, or what this creature is?"

Mr. Froze looks disgusted by the pictures, along with the other members as he replies sternly,

"Yes, okay, we will send an investigator back with you. They will report back to us with their findings. Mr. Jorden, know this, if we get a report back, and there is nothing to warrant your actions here today… you will be reprimanded severely."

Mr. Jordan nods, and replies,

"Thank you. I can promise you this Mr. Froze, you will find this is NOT a lie! I will leave you to your other business, thank you for your time."

Mr. Froze leans to the woman next to him as she whispers in his ear before he responds,

"You're welcome, thank you for coming! The investigator should be there tomorrow."

Mr. Jordan smiles as he answers satisfied,

"Okay, thank you."

Mr. Jorden turns and walks out of the room, and once the door closes, Mr. Froze turns to the rest of his committee, looking hard at each person before sighing. Shaking his head slowly, as he looks down at the desk before speaking disheartened,

"This is truly a sad day for us all in this room. I was sworn to secrecy, but I cannot stand by and watch our biggest resource of tourism be trashed by this monster. I want you all to swear to secrecy. What I am about to tell you cannot leave your lips after you leave this room."

Everyone looks concerned as they turn between each other confused. After a couple of minutes of chatter amongst themselves, all respond,

"Yes, of course, we won't say anything."

Ms. Caser stands up, and asks concerned,

"What could possibly be so secret that we are omitted from this knowledge of a possible monster lurking in our beautiful waters?"

Mr. Froze rubs his brow frustrated, as he looks up at Ms. Caser, and responds quietly,

"Ms. Caser, I will get to that shortly. Since you all nodded and agreed. Both the U.S. and our Government have been watching an unknown creature, the one who has been sinking ships and leaving no trace of them. We have moved the shipping lanes to the north of where it had been. Now it appears to have moved towards the shores of Cancun. We had hoped it would move out to the middle of nowhere. I guess we were wrong. Terrible wrong."

Putting his face in his hands, as Mr. Stein asks curiously,

"What is it, this creature?"

Mr. Froze lifts his head, and gives it a shake, as he answers unsure,

"We do not know Gerald, all we know is this monster is big, I would guess probably more than a hundred feet long? I do have one radio message from the cargo ship Valtice! I will play it for you, but it goes no further than this room, or any of you!"

Everyone nods, and individual responds,

"Yes Sir, everything stays in this room."

Reaching into his bag, Mr. Froze pulls out a handheld recorder. Placing it on the table, thumbing the volume up, and hitting play.

"Mayday! Mayday! Coast Guard, cargo ship Die Hard is going down, huge tentacles wrapping around the ship. Their ship looks as if the hull is melting, we are less than a hundred meters away, and the smell is awful. Please send help, we are heading to pick up the survivors who are in the water. The ship is almost submerged, I can see a creature, and 'MY GOD' I thought it was a squid, this thing is no squid! The tentacle's from what I can see are at least ninety feet long, its head is more rounded, I cannot see any eyes, but there is an almost clear blob sitting on the surface…"

…Screaming heard in the background, alarms start going off. A man shouts,

"Captain, something is eating through the bulkhead, we must abandon ship, NOW Captain!"

"Mayday, we are going down to, I have a beacon signal set to go. The clear stuff is attaching to our ship it must be highly acidic. WATCH OUT…."

Screams of at least three men in between static and gnawing, then dead silence.

Mr. Froze lowers his head, as he replies angered,

"That is all we have, the signal continued for four minutes and twenty-three seconds before being lost. We had ships out there in six hours, there was nothing left, even with sonar we could not find anything. Yes, this thing could ruin tourism if we do not stop it. I know we cannot do anything drastic right now, not with this Canadian Biologist here, we have kept this secret from their government, out of respect for the families…they do not need to know how they died, just that we support them in their time of need."

Mrs. Sanders wipes her eyes, as she asks,

"Yes, I can see the predicament we are in, how long is this woman going to be here?"

Mr. Froze look across the room, and answers uncertain,

"I do not know, hopefully, she will leave soon, then we can try and destroy this thing once and for all!"

Mr. Sam responds eagerly,

"Yes, if you would like Mr. Froze, we can come up with a battle plan for after she leaves, so we can hit right away?"

Mr. Froze nods slightly, as he answers,

"Perhaps that is what we should do. I will put all of our resources into destroying this monster! If possible, have this plan of yours on my desk in three days!"

Mr. Sam smiles, and replies excitedly,

"Yes, Sir! We will have this on your desk as quickly as we can. We'll make sure everything would be ready to go anytime you give the word!"

Placing his hands together in front of his face, Mr. Froze nods in approval before getting up.

Jantid

#6

Bobby, and Julie, young siblings running along the beach playing tag. Rex, their Xoloitzcuintli dog runs past them quickly, heading towards the water, and stops at the water's edge. Rex starts growling, barking loudly, as he stares. As the growls become more aggressive, the children make their way over to their dog. Julie rubs Rex's head a few times, while Rex continues staring into the ocean aggressively, barking as if he sees something. Julie looks out onto the water, not seeing anything she begins talking to Rex.

"What is going on Rex? Come on boy, let's go."

Grabbing Rex by the collar, they both begin forcefully pulling Rex away from the edge of the water, as Rex breaks out of their grasp, and begins barking more viciously, they turn to where Rex is, looking again. This time seeing a whale making weird painful noises, as they watch it struggle. Bobby and Julie follow Rex to the water's edge again. Watching in amazement as a sperm whale screams in pain, only twenty-feet out. This huge whale with tentacles wrapped around it. The whale screams out one last time as it begins bleeding out of its side, a giant weird beaked mouth emerges revealing endless rows of teeth. Julie and Bobby start screaming frightened. As the last of the whale disappears into the monster's mouth.

Rex begins whimpering and growling. As the mass begins moving closer to where the children are, Rex begins running around, and away from Julie and Bobby as they run further on the beach. Hiding behind a set of boulders, listening to Rex's barks turning into pained yelps. Julie peeks around the side then begins screaming at the top of her lungs.

"REX!"

Rex comes running back limping and yelping, hearing a tremendous splash, Julie grabs their dog, looking at this huge blob of monster sitting in only a few feet of water, tentacles thrashing around furiously. A brownish colour with a circular mouth with rows of razor-sharp teeth. Bobby turns to Julie, and shouts scared,

"What should we do Julie?"

Julie's looking at Rex's hind leg, blood trickling onto the sand, as she yells concerned,

"I do not know Bobby? We should get out of here, Rex is hurt pretty bad."

Bobby continues watches, as this beast thrashes around angrily, as he watches the creature inch onto the beach. Bobby hurriedly turns, and shouts,

"You take Rex home, I'll stay here and watch to see what it's going to do next?"

Julie nods, as she looks at Bobby one more time, and yells worriedly,

"Do not go near it, mom will be mad."

Bobby continues to watch it from only twenty-feet away, as he responds sarcastically,

"I promise not to go near it, okay?"

Julie grabs Rex's collar as they begin heading for their home. Once Julie's out of sight, Bobby watches the monster calm down. Grabbing a nearby stick, and picking up a few rocks. Bobby starts creeping within ten-feet of this monster. Chucking a rock at it as it puffs up a little. It becomes a darker brown color and begins squirming around again. Bobby steps closer, holding the stick in front of him, watching the movements of this creature. Stepping into the water, within five feet of it, Bobby begins screaming in agonizing pain, as the milky white strings floating in the water, coming from the monster, and latch on to Bobby's ankles. Bobby falls and a tentacle comes from behind him, wrapping around Bobby's waist to his feet. As Bobby's pulled towards the monster's mouth, it puffs up even more, revealing a jagged opening that shows teeth. A huge beaklike object appears to be emerging from the top of the opening of its mouth. Bobby's screams get muffled when the beast closes its beak and retracts. The monster takes itself down to water level again, as it pushes off the sand, and begins descending into the ocean once again.

#7

Standing by Jade's boat, Janice is getting ready for day one of the search for Jantid, a name given to this creature by Jade, and Janice last night. The sun shining brightly and clear waters should make it easy to find. As Janice, and Jade, begin to boarding the boat, Janice rubs her hand softly across the side of the boat and responds curiously,

"Is this a rubber of some sort?"

Jade stops, and turns around smiling, as she answers seamlessly,

"Yes, a synthetic rubber. A variation of sonar deflection rubber, along with top secret components. This way if Jantid's using a special kind of sonar to find his prey, especially with metal ships. Accordingly, he should not be able to find us, or at least he shouldn't?"

Janice continues to run her hand along the rails, as she answers softly,

"Well, that makes me feel safer. Where are we going to head first?"

Jantid

Jade puts a small metal suitcase by the bench, as she responds quietly while standing up straight and turning slightly as she catches something out of the corner of her eyes,

"Yes, as safe as it gets, I am thinking, we will head to where there is no fish. If what you told me about the fish beaching themselves is correct, plus in the wake of these other incidents, we should have a good shot of knowing where it may be hiding?"

Janice grabs another case and hands it to Jade, as she replies laughingly,

"Okay, you set the course and I will watch. Ha-ha!"

Jade grins, as she places the case down, and answers loudly,

"Aye, aye Captain Janice. Ha-ha!"

Laughter heard by the people standing at the pier, as the boat engine revs up and begins to back away from the dock slowly. Turning once it clears the pier, Jade hits forward, and the boat propels forward to head out to open water. As the five people on the boat begin reading the equipment. Once in open water, they drop the sonar and cameras. As the boat travels smoothly along the coastline. Jade fiddles with switches and knobs, there is a constant bleeping coming from the sonar, as Jade looks and responds,

"I'm thinking he may have moved further out to sea, there are several hundred fish in the area."

Janice looks a little relieved, as she glances over the side of the boat, and answers,

"I am glad of that, the further away Jantid is, the safer the people at the resort are."

Jade continues to fiddle with the switches, as she responds,

"Yes, but on the other hand, the deeper he is, the less chance we have of finding him."

Janice shakes her head, as she answers,

"Oh shoot, I forgot about that, hopefully, he is not too far away?"

After a few hours of trolling the waters, and no signs of anything. Suddenly the sonar goes crazier than ever beeping. Jade quickly looks into the scope, as huge schools of small and large fish shoot towards the shore frantically. Jade turns a dial, as the scope changes its direction, now looking the opposite way as the school of fish are headed, and responds concerned,

"Wow, look at them move, Jantid must be nearby."

Janice turns to look the same direction, as Jade, picking up a pair of binoculars. Janice takes a look through the binoculars, watching these fish zooming by and skimming the surface of the water. Turning towards Jade, as she replies concerned,

"I would say so, just looking over the side here, some are barely in the water."

Looking towards the onslaught of fish hitting the boat as they move at top speeds by the boat. As fish begin, floating around the side of the boat from knocking themselves out, the motors turned off, and the boat begins to drift along. The sonar continues going off like crazy. In the distance, a whale is seen moving in another direction, looking into the water after hearing a huge thud, and seeing a dolphin just floating there. Looking at it floating motionless, the sonar is now one long loud beep.

Jantid

Something dark begins turning the clear blue water, a dark brown shade. A figure of something begins emerging underneath the dolphin. Almost transparent tentacles begin floating all around the dolphin, which it starts making a pained squealing sound, and tries to move as a brown larger tentacle wraps around the dolphin and drags it under the water. As the grey silhouette disappears in what could be a mouth of sorts? Moving towards the shoreline. As Janice looks and shouts,

"Holy shit! That thing is huge, look at the sonar, it is still moving under the boat."

Jade hurriedly covers Janice's mouth with one hand, as she places the other over her own lips and whispers,

"Quieter please. Yeah, he is larger than I remember, let's check the monitor and see what he looks like now."

Janice nods slowly, as Jade removes her hand looking over the side of the boat. Janice quietly replies,

"Oh sorry, I forgot you put camera's down under the boat as well."

Walking over to the monitor, and clicking it on, a blank screen, then a clear blue picture. Rewinding the tape to three minutes earlier, catching the moment the dolphin hit the boat. A moment later, catching the barely seeable tentacles heading for the dolphin. Jantid's enormous body begins to rise from the depths in a sluggish majestic way. The blue water becomes a dark brown then blackish shadow, as the camera just catches the part that is touching the camera. After a bit, the camera is facing the bottom of the boat and is twisting around.

As the camera spins, it catches Jantid on every swirl around. Jade shakes her head, and responds,

"He must be way over a hundred feet long if we stop the footage at what looks like he is fifty feet away from the boat. … We should be able to infer his size…?"

Jade begins mumbling numbers, as she works out the math, then replies loudly covering her own mouth,

"Shit! If I did the math correctly, he is ninety-eight feet wide."

Janice looks amazed, as she replies dumbfounded,

"You're kidding, right? I mean how could no one not see him coming?"

Jade starts thinking, as she stares at the monitor, and responds,

"You're right. Perhaps I am looking at this the wrong way. Let's head back in."

As the motor revs up once again, turning the boat around, and following Jantid, staying a safe distance back, but being able to make him out in the monitor. Traveling at about ten knots, expanding and collapsing as he goes. After an hour of following, Jantid begins descending, as he continues forward, those transparent tentacles following behind continue to stay in view, as he disappears into the abyss. Jade yells out,

"Turn hard right!"

Janice worriedly yelps,

"What is happening?"

Jade points to the mass of clear tentacles, as she responds alarmed,

"I just realized something; I don't want to hit those clear tentacles. I believe those transparent tentacles are how it knows its prey are around. Like a jellyfish, they just float in the current. They probably sense the fish, or boats that touch them. Which in turn brings the rest of him to the surface."

Jim smiles, and nods, as he answers,

"Yes, of course, Jade, and when he comes up, the fish all scatter and it probably follows the bigger prey."

Jade grins, as she continues to watch the monitor for any movement while she answers,

"I think, perhaps you mean the ones closer, otherwise it would have gone for the whale."

Jim stops, and thinks for a moment, as he replies,

"Oh, yes, too excited. Sorry, Jade."

Janice giggles, Jim laughs, and Jade holds back, as she replies,

"No problem Jim. Now let's get back to shore and see if we can catch him at his own game?"

#8

As evening approaches and men search for Bobby Tamm's, after he was reported missing by his mom Betty. After Julie explained what happened to Rex and that Bobby stayed behind, the police pretty much figured out what happened. Not wanting to upset Betty anymore then she already is, they search in hopes of giving her a solid answer. After endless hours and no new clues, the police begin posting warnings, (Do not go near the water if you see the following, large numbers of fish near shore, or there is a blob that may resemble a Jellyfish, or Squid. By order of the Police Department.)

A meeting convenes at the resorts dining hall including members of the police department. Everyone is highly agitated by the police demands to stay out of the waters until this menace is taken care of.

As the want-to-be heroes comes sneaking out of the meeting, talking about killing the creature and saving the day. Joel, Greg, and Tom head to Bill's house since he has been fishing for some of the ocean's biggest predators. As they drive along the highway to Bill's house, away from civilization. Arriving there some two hours later, reaching a fence post with a freshly killed snake hanging on it. Driving onto the bumpy dirt road as dust begins flying, coming to a rickety old house with a flickering porch light. Coming to a stop by the front door, an Oldman in his sixty's, hair as wild and tangled as any jungle comes out holding a shotgun towards them. Tom holds his hands up, as he shouts terrified,

"Whoa! Bill, it's just some friends, Joel, Greg, and Tom."

Bill glares at the men, as he slightly lowers his shotgun, and angrily yells,

"What the hell brings you all out here?"

Joel, lowers his hands slowly, as does Greg, while Tom explains,

"We have a problem, Bill. We are hoping you can help us out?"

Bill grimaces, as he stares at the trio standing by his porch, like puppies looking for food. He spits off to the side, and responds,

"Must be a bad one huh? You would never have come this far otherwise. Go on… tell me, what is stuck in your backsides?"

The four of them sit down on the porch, all facing Bill with a distressed look on their faces, as Joel begins speaking worriedly,

"…Well, Bill, it is like this…there is a creature out there, or rather near the shores killing people. We want to stop it before it kills even more people…Bill… I know you used to kill all kinds of predators in your day. We are hoping you can help us out?"

Bill's eyes scan each of them, as he ponders for a while. He finally responds interested,

"Predator eh? What kind of predator are we talking here? I have wrangled many a creature, but there has always been a cost. Everything has a cost, seven years ago was the last time I paid the dearest price of all. My son Jack was with me, together we were a hunting machine, and nothing escaped our grasp!"

Wiping his eyes, as he stops, and takes a moment to remember his son Jack. After a moment of looking up at the night sky, he sighs, and continues explaining,

"We were hunting sharks along the coastline, removing them for the oil company. We had bagged our seventy-third one, in forty-five days. Working on the next one, this one bigger than the rest, least by a good ton. We fought that bastard for a good fifteen hours, we could see her shadow just below the light of the morning's sun. Bout another hour past I could see the beast estimating me. She was mere meters from being number seventy-four. Jack had the line tight, that shark was not going anywhere. That beast was thrashing round like no other…bout that time is when it was time to pay the reaper, cause that is when that beast leaped out of the water…took my son to the depths of the darkest hell. I only have that lasting memory of Jack, that shark took everything from me. After I came back. I sold the boat, and have never set foot on another since. I do not know what help I can offer you all?"

Joel leans forward, as he sorrowfully asks,

"Sorry for your loss Bill. Can you give us some advice, perhaps on what we can do to kill this monster?"

Bill ponders that question, as he stares at them intrigued. He points to some food on a plate and asks,

"…hmmm! What do you know about this creature of yours? Do you know what it feeds on? Is it a local, or does it migrate?"

Greg shakes his head unsure, as Tom answers,

"Seems to feed anytime and is large. I would say this beast migrates, as I have never seen anything like what they're talking about at the town meeting."

Bill looks at Tom hard, and states,

"You've not seen this creature you're looking to get? Well then, I guess…perhaps you should get yourself a boat, a big one. Find out what it eats, and go out there with everything you got. Guns, explosives, and anything else you can cause when it's time to pay the reaper, there ain't nothing that is going to help you."

Tom nods worried, as he looks towards Greg and Joel. Looking back at Bill, as he asks,

"Can you at least help us find a decent sized boat?"

Bill smiles a half tooth grin, as he answers,

"I could. There is a man I know, Devon, he might loan you his- - his leg was broken a couple of weeks ago, when he slipped on the deck. I will give him a call, he only lives a couple miles down the road."

Watching as Bill gets up, Joel, Greg, and Tom look at each other bewildered and excited, as Bill slams the screen door behind himself. Bill picks up the phone, calls his friend Devon, a lengthy conversation ensues. Greg gets up and starts pacing around as if something is gnawing at him. Tom begins chewing his nails, and Joel sits there running his fingers across his face nervously. After a half hour, Bill comes out of his house. Glaring at every one of them. They look worried as Bill shouts,

"Got you a damned boat! Now I want you all to listen to me…listen well! You will not come back here. Do not tell me any sob story that you, or you, or even you died! That is between you, and whomever you believe in. I have my own pile to cry on. Devon wants ten thousand a day that is the best I could get for you. You pay him, it is yours, and if you don't- -not my problem. Here is his address, now git!"

Tom, Greg, and Joel look at each other bewildered, as Tom replies,

"Umm, okay Bill, thank you."

As they walk back to their car, they take one last look back at Bill, who is standing there holding his gun again. About halfway up the road, a loud bang is heard. Joel turns to Greg, and responds,

"You don't think that came from Bill's place? Do you?"

Tom looks worried, as he replies unsure,

"No, maybe he was shooting at something?"

Turning on the main road heading to the address Bill gave them. Five minutes go by, and they reach a well-kept yard, with a silhouette of a huge boat bobbing up in down in the tide. Pulling up beside an SUV, and getting out. A man in his early forties, clean-shaven and dressed well comes out, a smile on his face. He holds out his hand as he responds kindly,

"You must be Greg, Tom, and Joel if I am right?"

Greg smiles, as he shakes Devon's hand, and replies,

"Yes, I am Greg, you must be Devon?"

74

Devon smiles, as he shakes Tom, and Joel's hands, and responds,

"Of Course. I am assuming Bill mentioned what the agreement involves for the boat?"

Joel nods, as he looks at the boat bobbing in the distance, and answers,

"Yes, we thought we could go into town in the morning, and withdrawn the funds."

Devon looks at them, as he responds,

"Do you carry credit cards? If you do, I have a machine inside, I do boat charters as well."

Tom, Joel, and Greg all nod, as Joel responds,

"Yes, we do, that would be great. So then we can set out right away?"

Devon looks at them strangely, and then his watch, as he responds,

"Yes...I guess we can, I was expecting to get some rest first."

Tom looks at the others as he thinks for a second, and replies,

"...Oh, you're coming with us? I thought we were going alone."

Devon starts laughing, as he shakes his head no, and answers,

"No, after talking with Bill, he told me you are planning on killing a sea creature. There is a certain code, I live by, you can borrow my boat, but you borrow it with me! I have most everything loaded on the boat, but I lack the depth charges. We can pick some up from a friend of mine in the morning."

Tom looks worried, as he looks at the others, then Joel asks,

"Okay, could we rent a room for the night?"

Devon looks at them, and shakes his head, as he replies,

"No, but you are welcome to stay in the guest bedrooms."

Tom looks relieved, knowing his wife would kill him for doing this. Greg responds,

"Okay, that would be great, thank you, Devon."

Heading into the house, everyone sits around the table talking and laughing. After about an hour, the laughter turns to planning how to stop this creature. Drawing pictures of what it may look like. Finally, everyone heads to their perspective rooms and all the lights go out.

Jantid

#9

Moonlight shimmering off the ocean, creating a rippling glow off the coast of Cuba just before dawn. Karl and his brother Jim set out to troll for fish. The low hum of their motor is the only sound to be heard. Using a spotlight to lead their way, they continue into the darkness. Dropping a net into the water and slowly moving along in their twenty-foot boat. Jim lights a cigarette as they patiently wait for the fish to swim into their trap, and become tangled up in their net. After waiting a good thirty minutes, they both begin pulling in their net. Hearing a splash in the distance, they begin pulling in a little faster, knowing the sharks will soon be looking for their breakfast.

Pulling fish out of the net as they come in, the net becomes heavy, almost pulling the brothers into the water. Bewildered by the weight of what may be in the net, the brothers struggle to pull it in. They mumble between each other, as they pull, hoping this is the big fish they have been looking for all year. The boat rocks back and forth violently while the brothers hold on for dear life. Their spotlight catches a tentacle breaching the water near the boat. Jim grabs a club and readies to smack it once it is in full sight. A few minutes pass as they tire from the hour-long struggle. As the squid flails around viciously, Jim raises his right hand, swinging the club a few times as water splashes, and the sound of the squid banging the wooden boat hard echoes loudly. (Laughing) as they pull the squid into the boat, along with the rest of the net in with their catch. Jim whacks the squid a few more times, as it starts moving again. Karl sits down to rest for a minute, rubbing his hands from where the net was digging in.

They begin heading back inland, as the sun begins brightening the morning sky. Jim starts separating the different fish species. They reach the shore and wave to other fishermen just heading out. Dragging their boat up onto the beach. Karl puts a wooden crate on the sand and begins dumping fish into it. Grabbing a tarp, the brothers roll what looks like the most screwed up squid they'd ever seen out of their boat. They haul the fish while dragging the squid to the marketplace.

Walking over to Hahn, a short stout man whose attitude can change in the blink of an eye. Hahn stares at the two men intensely, as they approach him. They stop in front of the man who buys their catches. Hahn begins looking through the fish but stops when he gets to the six-foot squid, glancing up at Karl, and Jim shaking his head annoyed, as he states angrily,

"What the heck is this supposed to be? A defective squid or something? Does not look right? I hope you two aren't trying to scam me…? I'll make sure you sell nothing here again!"

Karl sees the look on Hahn's face, turning towards the funny looking squid, then back at Hahn, Gulping as he quickly responds,

"No, not at all Hahn! We would never do anything like that to you. I do not know what happened to it, but it put up a good fight. Ha-ha!"

Karl tries to convincingly laugh, as Hahn glares at them both disappointed, while he points to the fish and squid stating irritated,

Jantid

"I will take the fish, but I do not know about this thing? I have never seen a squid with so many anomalies before? This is just a blob with no eyes, and those clear tentacles coming out of its mouth. They look like they belong to a jellyfish or something. Let us see if it ate one?"

As Hahn puts on his rubber gloves, and reaches in, and pulls back the slimy stinking mess until he reaches where the beak should be. He rummages around with a puzzled expression on his face. Placing his left hand on the beast's large brown tentacle, he grasps onto one of the semi-clear tentacles and tugs hard. Shaking his head, as he responds madder,

"This monstrosity has no beak that I can feel. Whatever those tentacles are, they belong to this creature. This is no squid, it has the basic shape of a jellyfish, so unless a squid mated with a jellyfish, you have garbage here, and it's not worth a dime to me."

Jim looks over at Karl, then Hahn, as he responds confused,

"Don't lie, Hahn, it has to have a beak. I swear I saw one before I whacked it across the head."

Shrugging his shoulders as he looks at them, and begins splitting open its mouth wider, so they can see inside, Hahn swears while pulling his hand out bleeding,

"Damn thing has teeth. Let me use these spreaders. I'll be right back."

Jim watches as Hahn walks over to the wall, and grabs a pipe-like object off, and brings it over, handing the pipe to Jim, as Hahn states,

"I want you to pry its mouth open, as wide as possible, can you do that?"

Jim looks at Hahn's face, as he answers cautiously,

"Yes, I will do it."

Hahn pulls the device across the opening of its mouth, as Jim begins cranking, and the mouth opens revealing teeth upon teeth. Hahn begins talking, and pointing,

"You see how its mouth opens, and those teeth are curving into its own mouth like they are, this is a super predator. No beak, this is an evolutional squid, a beak is good for quickly devouring their prey, in little portions. These teeth are razor sharp, and curved. This squids designed to latch on and pull the food in, possible snapping their prey in half. I do not get the Jellyfish tentacles though? Unless… they are meant to paralyze their victim? I think you two may have discovered a new species of squid. A new, and even more dangerous species. I will let you store it here if you want to go find a reporter willing to come here, and do a story about it? Perhaps, you'll be paid for this squid yet?"

Jim looks amazed, as he smiles and responds excitedly,

"Do you think so, Hahn?"

Hahn looks at the creature, and shakes his head slightly stating,

"I do not know if you will or not? Find a reporter, and bring him back here, you will know then."

Jantid

#10

Jade comes walking onto the deck wearing a red t-shirt, white shorts. Stretching her arms towards the sky. Walking towards Janice sitting on a bench, wearing a blue bikini, lost in thought, holding her coffee. Standing next to her, finally tapping on Janice's shoulder. Making her jump, as she turns towards Jade, with a confused look. Jade smiles back, and responds happily,

"Sorry, I didn't see you were entranced with the view so deeply."

Jade glances around while Janice, giggles as she answers,

"No worries, I must have been daydreaming, I guess I must have lost myself. Ha-ha!"

Jade continues to look at the sea smiling, as she replies,

"Yes, the view is extraordinary, from the sun beginning its rise. I have looked upon mornings for almost three years all over the world. Nothing better than here though."

Sitting down beside Janice, they watch, as the sun becomes broader in the sky. Jade turns to Janice slowly, and asks,

"You said you were daydreaming about something? May I ask what it was?"

Janice smiles, as she looks towards Jade and replies,

"Oh, yes of course. I was thinking about yesterday…what if the reason it dived was to get behind us. I do not mean literally, but what if it sensed the boat was following him?"

Jade begins thinking, as she sits playing with her cup, and responds thoughtfully,

"I know, I thought the same thing, which is why I made sure Jim turned the boat away. I personally believe those almost transparent strings are its eyes. Most squid have eyes I did not see one. I checked the video after everyone went to bed, not once did an eye ever appear in view."

Janice sits forward quickly, and responds,

"You know, I never thought about that before. Therefore, I wonder if it lets those things rise up in the water. Something swims by, touches them, Jantid rises to the surface, and gives chase. Sending thousands of fish sprawling to get out of its way, or become his supper?"

Jade smiles at Janice, and replies knowingly,

"Exactly! Without them, it may be blind and unable to sense what is around it. What I am thinking today? If we go out to where we were, we try to get a piece of those tentacles. Bring it back to the lab, and examine it thoroughly."

Janice grins, as she looks at the sun shining between a series of trees near the top of the pier, then turns to Jade, and replies,

Jantid

"Yeah, that would be a great start. I cannot believe we did not think of it yesterday."

Jade kind of smiles, as she answers,

"I can tell you that, I was not planning to grab anything from him, I just wanted to make sure Jantid was not going to sink this boat. After all the ships he has sunk, I wanted to make sure this investment was well worth the cost, before committing to the open water, and yesterday, I learned it was worth every penny. This rubber coating saved us, bigtime."

Janice looks shocked, as she stares at Jade, confused, while she responds,

"Oh, really? Why would you do something like that without telling anyone?"

Jade touches Janice's hand lightly, and looks apologetic, as she replies,

"I'm sorry, but I had to know Janice. You see, if we do not destroy it, we need to find a way to ensure ships can safely pass by without losing their cargo. Last year alone, Jantid globally cost companies hundreds of billions of dollars. I hope we can destroy Jantid, because, if we let him live, he could deplete the entire food chain of the ocean in a matter of years…less possibly?"

Janice smiles again, nodding, as she answers agreeing,

"I see what you mean, yeah that makes sense, well if we can get one of those tentacles, perhaps we can figure out a weakness for him?"

Jade pats Janice's leg softly, and replies,

"I am sure we will Janice. Everything has something that affects them immensely."

Janice leans forward, as an engine of a small boat comes cruising towards Jade's boat. Janice taps Jade's arm, and asks,

"Jade, who is this coming towards your boat?"

Jade stands up quickly, as the boat comes closer, she answers puzzled,

"...I don't know? Well, let's see what they want?"

Watching as the boat makes its way towards Jade's docked boat, and slows down. The one man kills the engine, and the boat starts drifting within twelve-feet. A well-dressed man in a navy blue suit waves with a grin on his face. Roger Sage, a man in charge of tourism yells,

"Excuse me? I am looking for a Jade Mills, is she aboard?"

Staring at this man, Jade looks annoyed, as she responds,

"You found her, who are you?"

Roger grins, as he replies,

"Ah, good. My name is Roger Sage, I am here on behalf of the Mexican government, and they want me to help you, looking into what is happening in the waters here."

Jade looks puzzled after he says this, turning towards Janice, as she grabs her badge from her purse, and stands up, responding loudly,

"I see, well Mr. Sage, I'm Janice Tore's, and the local police are in charge of this investigation. If you go a ways over there, I am sure another police officer will be able to help you."

Roger shakes his head no, as he responds,

"I do not think you understand, I am here to accompany 'you' I have talked with the police officer in charge. Frank Jordan, and he said you are in charge of this operation."

Jade watches, as the boat creeps closer to her boat. She holds her hands up aggressively, and shakes her head (No), as she answers angrily,

"I am sorry, but I cannot allow you to board. You will have to discuss this with my office Mr. Sage."

Roger's taken aback, as he looks at the captain of his boat bewildered, and replies,

"You are not allowing me aboard? After you've been given permission to dock here! This is an outrage! I will not tolerate this kind of behavior."

Jade grabs a card from her jacket pocket hanging by the door. Reaching over, as Roger reaches as well, and barely grabs the card, as Jade responds,

"Here is my card, you give that number a call, and they will tell me what to do. My hands are tied until then Mr. Sage."

Roger looks at the card angrily, as he shouts,

"I assure you Ms. Mills, I will be back, and soon."

Mr. Sage gets his boat quickly to the closest pier. As the boat takes off to the pier about a hundred feet away, Jade turns to Janice, and responds,

"I bet you are wondering about that? Yes, there is equipment on this boat that is way ahead of the times. These devices are capable of starting wars. No government officials allowed to board this boat, not even the American government. This is strictly for marine biology 'only' and if a government were to use it the wrong way, they could actually start world war three. I have a device for underwater use only. This sends a beam in every direction possible. If someone were to take it to full power, everything in a seven hundred mile radius in the water including subs would be, fried. Not to mention the water temperature would rise a good thirty degrees! Who knows what changes would happen, to the wildlife here, probably all die! That is the only reason there are no Government official's allowed."

Janice looks dumbfounded, as she struggles to find the words, as she responds worried,

"Holy! I get what you are saying, something like that defiantly would interest them."

Jade looks at Janice, and smiles, as she holds her shoulder, and states,

"Yes, now before he gets back here, let's get this boat out of here."

Janice gets up, and runs to the bow, as Rick unties the boat from the dock. Janice pulls up the rope. Jade runs to the stern and begins hauling up the rope, Rick, and Jim both jump on, as the boat begins to drift. Jim runs into the wheelhouse, the engine roars to life, a puff of black smoke rises. The boat begins to move out into the harbor. As the boat pushes forward, Mr. Sage comes running, his hands waving frantically trying to get them to stop. His voice barely audible in the wake of the engines roar. Mr. Sage stands there looking furious, "What the Hell?" He finally becomes little more than a fleck of dust while everyone begins turning on the equipment. Afterwards Janice looks over at Jade, and shakes her head worried, as Jade turns, and replies,

"I had no choice. If he had gotten on, they would seize the boat for carrying weapons. Even though these are not weapons. After we deal with today, trying to get a specimen to analyze. We will switch boats. I have another one that looks the same. Has the same name too, I will take the heat for anything that happens from that incident."

Janice looks astonished, as she looks back towards the pier, and answers boldly,

"Well you are brave, aren't you Jade. I would have just let him on board."

Jade grins a knowing smile, as she responds,

"No, you wouldn't Janice. If you had what is on here, and knew what it was capable of, you would do exactly what I did. I do not see you as a person willing to sacrifice your morals for politics'."

Janice, looks thoughtful, as she watches Jade, getting Jim to speed up a bit more. Janice sighs, and replies,

"I guess you're right, I would not have let him aboard either."

Jade walks back over to Janice, looking her in the eyes, as she states confidently,

"Do not worry about anything, nothing is going to happen to you. You have my word as a human being."

As everyone goes about their business, Rick looks through the binoculars, looking surprised as he sees, Mr. Sage in the distance on a speedboat, and starts calling out to Jade anxiously,

"We have company! That guy is coming towards us, what do you want us to do?"

Jade runs over to where Rick is pointing, as he passes the binoculars to her. Looking through them, as she responds,

"Oh, he is coming again… well, I guess he will have to return to land. Make sure to raise the side's three-feet. That should deter him a little bit."

Janice looks confused, as she asks questioningly,

"Raise the sides?"

Jade hands the binoculars back to Rick, as she turns to Janice, and replies cunningly,

"Oh yes, this boat is meant for hard seas, therefore the sides raise to prevent flooding on the deck."

Just as Jade finishing talking, a sonic boom of an explosion crosses their ears, making them all quickly turn in the direction of the sound as Janice holds her chest, and fearfully asking,

"What the hell was that? Was that an explosion?"

Jantid

#11

Devon sits at the table, drinking coffee, and has just finished eating his breakfast. Looking at his watch, shaking his head, as he waits for Greg, Tom, and Joel to come join him. Frustrated, getting up and walking to their rooms banging on each door until he hears an answer. Going back to finish his coffee. Another five minutes go by before he sees them emerging from their rooms. Devon grimaces, as he states angrily,

"I thought you fellows wanted to get an early start, was I wrong Joel?"

Joel stands in the doorway rubbing his eyes, as he answers startled,

"No, what time is it anyways?"

Devon scowls at them, as he replies annoyed,

"Half past four! What is your term for early boys, noon?"

Tom looks worried, as he replies,

"Yeah, I usually get up at the crack of dawn."

Devon looks out the window and turns back to them, and sternly answers,

"Well dawn will be here in about another ten minutes. I usually like leaving before dawn, gives me a chance to know I am still alive."

After everyone quickly eats. Joel, Greg, and Tom get aboard the ship, as they begin to move out into the open water, the engine begins to rev up, and they head to pick up the depth charges. After an hour, they come to a small port where an elderly man is standing with crates beside him. Devon gets off the boat, and goes and talks to the man. Joel and his friends stand there watching. Devon and this man laugh while pointing out into the ocean. Finally, Devon is coming back aboard carrying a box. He looks at Joel sternly, and responds,

"Well, are you all going to stand there? Go get the rest of them boxes. You are not paying me to be your slave!"

Joel nods, as he replies dumbfounded,

"Yes, come on guys, let's do this!"

As Joel, Tom, and Greg haul the ten boxes aboard and then pay the man for the boxes. Once they are on their way again, Greg walks up to Devon, and asks inquisitively,

"What is in those boxes that cost five thousand dollars each?"

Devon looks at the boxes, as he responds irritated,

"You should know, those are the depth charges. Make sure you do not blow up my boat. Do you boys understand?"

Joel looks almost insulted, as he responds annoyed,

"We won't! How long before we find it?"

Devon glares at Joel, as he answers snarky,

"How the heck am I supposed to know that? I guess we will find it when we see it."

Joel looks at Tom, as he replies,

"Okay, I thought maybe you had an idea, where should we look first?"

Devon's face shows aggravation, as he responds at his wits end,

"I do. Out there, why do you not go join your friends at the bow and look for it?"

Joel looks at Devon's face and quickly replies.

"Yes, sir."

Greg walks out onto the deck as Devon shakes his head in disbelief, as he looks at the three of them trying to figure out what they are doing. Once it seems like they have something planned. They all begin trying to set the depth charges to different depths. Joel comes walking into the wheelhouse and asks,

"What depth are we at? So we can start dropping them?"

Devon looks worried, as he answers,

"About a twelve hundred feet so far. Do you people have a clue what you are doing with those? If not, I will give you a hand. I do not want my boat going down, do you understand?"

Joel nods, and answers confidently,

"We do Devon. We just want to make sure we set them at the right depth."

Looking still unsure about them doing it right, Devon answers,

"Make sure no less than seventy feet. That should be forty seconds. Make sure to set those timers for four-zero. No less."

Joel smiles excitedly, and responds,

"Got it, we will start dropping shortly."

Joel heads back outside with his friends; Devon begins to speed the boat up in hopes of not having his boat blown up. As he cringes while watching them begin throwing the depth charges over the side into the water. Twenty-five seconds after they throw them, a burst of water and an ear-shattering, Bang. Devon just looks back, the fear in his face, as if he knows this is going to be bad. Three minutes later, one goes off, super close. Devon yells out enraged,

"HEY WHAT THE HELL ARE YOU DOING GREG?"

Greg fearfully turns to look at Devon as he shouts apologetically,

"SORRY! That one would have been defective."

Devon glares at him closely, as he responds, and then mumbles,

"Maybe. Or maybe your heads defective… Christ!"

Looking forward and seeing a smaller boat approaching at a high speed. Devon blows the horn, but the boat is still on a collision course. Trying to turn the wheel, but it is jammed up. Devon hurriedly throws the engines in full reverse. Tom, Greg, and Joel jolt forward, almost going over the rail. Greg loses grip of the depth charge, as it goes flying into the wheelhouse unnoticed by Devon, as he yells,

"GOD DAMMNIT! GRAB ON TO THE RAILING! THAT BOATS GOING TO HIT US!"

The boat continues on its collision course, as it hits the boat, and explodes into flames. Greg shouts into Devon, as he tries getting to his feet,

"DEVON, THERE'S A DEPTH…"

Devon feels something hit his foot, and turns looking at Greg, with hatred in his eyes, as the wheelhouse explodes, sending Tom, Joel, and Greg flying into the water. Bobbing in the water, watching the two boats burn. Knowing the noise made by this explosion will attract some unwanted attention soon. Joel grabs Tom, who is bobbing unconscious face down. Greg comes swimming over to help hold Tom above the water.

Minutes pass before a shark fin appears near them. As the duo slap the water trying to get the shark to leave. Soon, more fins appear, getting closer at each pass. Within five minutes, the sharks become less interested in them, as Joel watches one shark quickly turn, and head into the darker water…

#12

Jade, Janice, Rick, and Jim look around, finally seeing a bulge of black smoke rising from the ocean. Jim points, and shouts, as he sees the billowing mass of black smoke,

"There it is Jade, over in the south!"

Jade and the rest turn towards the smoke, as Jade yells,

"Holy! We better head over there and see if we can help, Jim."

Jim nods, as he frantically shouts and runs to the wheelhouse,

"Yes, I will turn course!"

Jim grabs the wheel and starts turning to head towards the smoke, the speedboat pulls up beside them. Mr. Sage uses a megaphone, and begins talking angrily,

"Let me aboard now! I talked to them, and they said you must let me aboard."

Jade glares over at him, and responds angrier,

"They have not called me. I doubt very much they did tell you — you are welcome aboard."

Mr. Sage's angry expression, as he shouts,

"They did! ..."

Jade responds as she points towards the smoke cloud,

"Go back to land, we are trying to help another ship in distress, we can discuss this later Mr. Sage."

Mr. Sage gets more agitated by the second, as he yells,

"We can discuss this 'NOW', lower a line and pull me aboard."

Jade watches Mr. Sage closely, while leaning up against the rail, as she answers,

"Sorry, you can follow us if you like, but it will not change anything."

As the arguing continues between Jade and Mr. Sage, the boat begins to speed up. The speedboat turns and heads back to the harbor. As they continue to race over to where the smoke is coming from.

After an hour and a half, the boat comes upon floating debris, slowly drifting by, picking up items with a gaff. Sharks circling around, looking like they are waiting for a meal to drop in. After picking up everything that was floating around, everyone begins looking at the items. Janice looks at Jade, and states,

"Hey, there are two different ships here. This one is from Caitlyn's Dream, somethings cruise. I cannot make out the first part?"

Jade begins scanning nearby surroundings, as she answers,

"Okay, so I guess they must have collided, that would explain the explosion. I do not understand why there are bits of dead fish floating all around though? The sharks should have eaten them by now."

Jim looks over the items, and replies cautiously,

"Maybe a fishing boat?"

Jade turns to look at Jim, and the items laying on the deck. She ponders as she stares, then answers with certainty,

"No, these are fancy items, things you would not find on a fishing boat. If I had to guess…? Maybe one of the high-end boat charters in the area?"

Jim glances up at Jade, as he continues to pick through the items, and replies worried,

"Something bad must have happened, that was a huge explosion. Perhaps something chasing these boats?"

While discussing the items at hand, a beeping comes from the sonar and begins quickening ever so quickly. Standing straight up, Jade and Janice run inside to watch. Jade calls out to Jim,

"Jim! Drop the Camera into the water, and I mean NOW!"

Jim quickly runs over to a metal case, as he replies,

"Okay Jade, give me a second."

Jim hurriedly opens the metal case carrying the cameras, Jade looks out the window, seeing a giant fin coming towards them. Janice notices it too. Both of them stare as this fin goes by the boat. Turning to look out the other window, the fin begins to descend. The sonars still going crazy. Jim finally drops the camera down, as the monitor cracks to life. Watching as a picture appears, blurry, then clears up showing an eighteen-foot great white shark beginning to dive into the depths and fades into the darkness. The sonar keeps beeping; trying to swing the camera around, trying to catch a glimpse of what else is setting the sonar off. Catching only a shadow below. Jade replies unsure,

"Has to be that shark, nothing else that close by, which could be causing this sonar to go off this bad Janice?"

Janice continues to watch the screen and responds puzzled,

"Yeah, I cannot see anything either?"

"Okay, let us head out and try and find Jantid! Keep everything in the water. We should not have Mr. Sage following us."

The boat engine starts up and begins moving away from the area. A few hours of traveling provide nothing more than little blips on the screen. Picking up the phone, Jade makes a call to get the other boat ready, and waiting to go, at an assigned place. After hanging up, Jade looks at Janice and smiles while answering,

"No problem, everything is good to go! Mr. Sage will probably give me a headache, but otherwise, we should be fine."

After switching boats, Jade and the others begin making their way back to the harbor. The sun is setting, as they make their approach, the engines slowing to a crawl, as Jim, and Rick jump on the dock, grabbing the ropes Jade, and Janice through over, and tying the boat up. The engine stops, and Janice gets off, says her goodbyes, and heads on her way. Jim and Rick stick around for a while as they lock everything up. After an hour of making sure everything was secured, Jade, Jim, and Rick head into the resort for a good night's sleep.

#13

Non-stop banging on the hotel room door where Jade is staying. Getting out of bed, and walking over to the door. Opening it, and seeing Mr. Sage standing there, looking rather unhappy. Jade's smile is warm and welcoming as she responds kindly,

"Yes, can I help you Mr. Sage?"

Seeing her smile, almost enrages Mr. Sage, while he stares at Jade, he replies demandingly,

"Ms. Mills, after your disrespectfulness, I want aboard your boat, NOW!"

Jade leans against the door, just smiling, as she calmly responds,

"Okay, I will be there later today, around noon."

Mr. Sage's eyes intensify, as he replies loudly,

"No, you denied me on your boat yesterday! Against the wishes of my government…"

The smile comes off Jade's face, as she glares at Mr. Sage, with a cold stare, as he moves back slightly worried as Jade stands straight up, and steps closer to Mr. Sage, as she answers angrily,

"Look here, PAL! That is my boat out there, not your government's boat! I let whomever I want on it. Do not come here to MY room, and try to tell me 'I have to' or you can go to hell right now! I said I will be there at 'NOON!' alright Mr. Sage!"

Slamming the door closed in his face. Leaving Mr. Sage, enraged, turning around, staring at the many people who are now peering out of their rooms, staring at him. Walking away with a rather embarrassed look across his face, hurriedly walking to the elevator. As people just continue to stare at him a little longer and then begin closing their doors. An extremely angered look on his face, as he waits for the elevator while clicking the down button, rapidly.

As noon approaches, Mr. Sage is standing on the dock, glancing at his watch impatiently. Mumbling under his breath waiting for Jade to come. His ego still bruised from this morning's lashing. Jade, finally comes walking along the pier, a smile radiates off her, as her new purplish hair flows gently in the warm breeze. Mr. Sage hurriedly walks over to her, anger drooling from his lips, stopping a mere three feet from her. He looks at Jade's hair, as he angrily states,

"What? You stopped and got your hair done? I've been waiting here since eleven-thirty for you!"

Jade's smile fade, as she glares at him with distaste while answering,

"Yeah, I did! What concern is it of yours anyway? I said noon and it's ten to. You know, you seem to have quite an attitude, for someone who expects to be taken seriously. You know what forget it. I have serious business to attend to, trying to save people from being killed by this creature. I do NOT have time for these games your government are playing. Goodbye Mr. Sage."

Jade walks past Mr. Sage annoyed, as he takes a deep breath, and responds apologetically,

"…Wait, Jade…? I'm sorry about my attitude. I have been under a lot of pressure from my bosses. They want me to figure out what this sea monster is? Can we talk, on your boat?"

Jade turns around and stares at him for a minute. Finally, she replies annoyed,

"Fine, make it quick!"

As they both get on board Jade's boat, Mr. Sage's humbled facial expression says more than words ever could. As they sit down on a bench near the bow. Mr. Sage fiddles something small in his hands while lowering his head instead of looking Jade in the eyes. He takes a deep breath and begins speaking,

"I am sorry for everything that has transpired so far. My government has been trying to find ways of ridding our shores of this horrid beast. I should not be saying this to you, but we have a specimen, a smaller version of what we assume is out there. The one we have, 'dead' of course, was lethal at twelve inches."

Jade, ponders, as she hears this, considering the possibilities of more than one of these deadly creatures roaming around. Stuttering at the thought as she answers quickly,

"That means it is either a-sexual, or there are two of them? How long ago did you find that one your government captured, and where did you capture it?"

Mr. Sage looks Jade, directly in the eyes, as he replies,

"Four years ago I believe? A male swimmer washed up on shore, this very shore screaming in agony. They rushed him to the hospital where the man died shortly after being admitted. This abomination was still eating his leg, and it had been out of the water for at least half an hour by then. They tried to kill it, but it latched on to the doctor's arm, and the doctor died as well. After the toxicology report found a high amount of neurotoxins and radiation. We dissected it, we found that it has tentacles like a jellyfish. From what we could see, its teeth is how it ingests its victims, there was something weird though…? It has acid glands, we figured out that is how it has taken so many ships. It travels through the transparent tentacles. That is why I wanted on your boat so bad. I saw the rubber you have on yours. I figure your boat is the safest."

Jade, gives a look of concern, as she glances at Mr. Sage with a little apprehensiveness. Finally, she responds reserved,

"Yes it is, but this is only the testing period. From what you have told me about Jantid, this is what we have named it. If this thing can breathe in air, we could be in for even more fun. I was basing my conclusions on it being contained to the water. I am still working on a way to kill it, and now, I'll have to add this new information as well. How did your government manage to kill the small one?"

Mr. Sage quickly responds quietly,

"The way they finally killed it… antimatter … experimental antimatter!"

Jade looks shocked, as she shakes her head no, and replies quieter,

"Experimental antimatter? Holy, that must be rare to find, and expensive as hell. Are you sure that is what killed it?"

Mr. Sage nods, as he answers,

"Yes, we are quite sure, it shriveled up almost immediately."

Jade considers the applications and destructive nature of this, could it be possibly lethal to everyone antimatter? She looks intently, as she asks questioningly,

"How much did you have to use for it to be lethal to this creature?"

Mr. Sage thinks for a while before he replies,

"They used just over a gram, and that was given in increments, once it hit over a gram, that is when it died."

Jade still considers the effects on everyone and everything around the area. Jade looks down at the deck, as she replies inquisitively,

"I see, well if it works on the small ones, that big one would need over a hundred times that."

Mr. Sage looks Jade in the eyes, as he states sternly,

"Yes, at least that much. If you allow me to help, I guarantee you one hundred percent help from our government!"

Jade, nods slightly, as she considers making a deal with a possible devil? She replies hesitantly,

"Alright, together we will find a way to help each other. There is not much going on here today. By the looks of the beach, I am guessing the people are realizing something is going on here?"

Mr. Sage nods agreeing, as he responds,

"Yes, it was only a matter of time before this happened. People are not stupid when it comes to monsters such as this, once the signs are in place, all we can do is wait for the recoil."

Jade nods, as she replies assertively,

"Yes Mr. Sage, I have been trying to find this beast for years, it is extremely elusive. Now that I have some ideas of how to kill it, I just need to find enough antimatter to kill it. In addition, we have to hope it does not have any young out there?"

Mr. Sage, shakes his head, as he answers fearfully,

"Oh God, I would hate to think what would happen if there are more of them out there? I will make some calls and see about getting this antimatter. I will let you be for now, I know we are in two different professions, and I should not infer on yours any longer. Thank you for your hospitality Ms. Mills, and I am sorry about my attitude, it was uncalled for."

Jade smiles, as she responds humbly,

"Thank you, and I do apologize for mine as well."

Mr. Sage stands up, and bows slightly, as he responds,

"Not at all, you had every right to throw it back in my face. I must go now, thank you again for your time."

Mr. Sage holds his hand out, Jade holds her out, and they slowly shake hands. Mr. Sage walks off the boat and begins walking up the dock. Waving as he disappears in the distance. Jade looks around annoyed, something seems to be eating away at her. Finally, she begins looking around, dropping to her knees where Mr. Sage was sitting, a dull flashing light emanates from under the bench. Jade angrily grabs the tracker, and is ready to throw it overboard, then stops suddenly. Looking at it blinking, Jade gets a smile across her face, as she mutters,

"Son of a gun… I knew it."

Squeezing it tightly in her right hand, as she begins walking slowly over to the dockside of the boat. Jade, walks off the boat, onto the pier. Looking around the dock shaking her head frustrated. Grinning as the boat rubs up against the tire, tied to the dock. Glancing around mischievously, Jade pulls out a pocket knife. Kneeling down, and plunging the knife into the tire, twisting it slightly. Pulling the knife out, and carefully pushing the tracker into the cut. Pushing it gently in enough to hide it out of sight.

#14

On the Island of Cuba, in the fish market, Hahn has waited long enough for any reporter to show up. This creature has been stinking up his place since it came in yesterday morning. Grabbing a trolley, he heads to the freezer room. Hahn pulls the trolley up next to this creature, grabbing and pulling it onto the trolley with a loud thud. Covering his nose as he mutters,

"Holy cow! What is that smell?"

Grabbing the crate next to where he placed the squid, he takes a quick sniff and shakes his head annoyed. Placing the box on the trolley, he wheels it out to the trash, not being able to lift it, he pushes the beast off the trolley, onto the ground, and heads back inside to open up.

A few hours pass and people begin making their way in, for fresh fish or bring in catches. Business goes like every other day. Karl comes in around nine in the morning, walking up to Hahn, and asks,

"Morning Hahn, did Arnold come in yet?"

Hahn grimaces while stating angrily,

Jantid

"No! And I'm not too pleased with you, or your brother either. You left that putrid smelling piece of garbage to smell up my place of business. You two owe me fifty dollars' worth of fish because of that wretched thing."

Jim comes walking up just in time to hear Karl replying angrily,

"Fifty dollars? We never stole any fish from you!"

Hahn glares both of them down, as he answers aggressively,

"You didn't, but half a crate of fish is missing, and another box that was sitting above that, that… stinking monster ruined those fish, by the smell alone."

Jim holds his hands up in front of Hahn, trying to calm him down some. Hahn gets angrier, as he smacks Jim's hand away, and states loud enough, everyone in the fish market turns to look,

"I still have them out back! Come with me and I'll show you what damage that monstrosity caused to me."

Hahn turns, and walks to the back of the building, Jim, and Karl, follow behind him concerned and worried. Hahn stops outside, covering his nose as he continues speaking loudly,

"You take a whiff of this… godawful… makes me want to puke! You two are no longer welcome here… you leave now, and take that whatever it is with you. You pay me fifty dollars, then you can come back. Not before though!"

Before either of the brothers can say anything, Hahn darts back inside, getting away from the smell of the monstrosity that sits behind his building unthawing as the morning progresses. Jim and Karl turn away from yesterday's catch disgusted by the smell emanating from it. Karl responds frightened,

"We are going to have to pay Hahn, or we're in real trouble if we can't sell our catches to him."

Jim nods agreeing, as he answers,

"Yes! Let's see if we can scrape up that kind of money."

The two brothers run down the alley, as Hahn comes walking back ready to yell at them some more. Sticking his head out the door, he looks around annoyed, as he glances down at the squid and shakes his head angrily, he turns to head back in, all the while mumbling to himself.

A loud crashing noise turns everyone's heads to the back of Hahn's fish market. Hahn quickly makes his way to the back, he walks out by the garbage cans. Looking around, noticing that that creature is missing, he begins digging through the garbage then stops suddenly. Hearing a gurgling sound coming from behind him catches him off guard, slowly he begins turning around. Seeing the creature behind him, with its mouth open, standing three-feet tall.

He lets out a short-lived scream, as the tentacles wrap around him and squeeze tight. Hahn turns blue as this beast's mouth opens up wide. Hahn's eyes bulge, as he watches in horror, as a beak comes out on the outer side of its teeth. Pulling Hahn towards its mouth. Hahn's pained expression says it all, as the beak snaps closed on his stomach. His eyes close while he goes limp and stops struggling. Blood and body parts pool at Hahn's feet, as the tentacles latch onto Hahn, and drag him inside his mouth.

Soon another man comes out and begins striking it with a shovel, a squishing sound is all it makes, a transparent tentacle gets caught on the shovel as the man brings it back for another hit. The tentacle let's go and drops across the man's face, as he screams in pain, and tries to get it off, causing himself more pain as he falls to the ground, holding his face, as it moves towards the man. A brown tentacle grabs him and begins pulling him towards its widening mouth. He screams louder.

Everyone comes running upon hearing his screams, they stop short, as they see this horror unraveling in front of them. Some begin trying to run past it, as it makes loud gurgling noises. Others scatter back into the building screaming. Some people manage to avoid the flailing tentacles, and slip away, while others slip and fall on the slimy tentacles. Within moments, the fish markets cleared out, except for the ones who are now caught in the various tentacles screaming in agony. Within minutes, all the voices of the people caught fall silent. The creature begins making its way to the ocean again.

#15

Jade, and Janice, along with Rick, and Jim have been searching non-stop for hours, not a signal from anything but the fish swimming by. Jade addresses everyone in front of her by responding,

"Hey, I am going to throw a thought out here. Two days, we haven't seen Jantid, I am wondering if it may have moved to a new location, what do you all think?"

Janice contemplates for a moment, then responds,

"I do not know about Jim or Rick, but I think it's still here. I know, I am not experienced like you are, but there are an abundant amount of fish, and people, so why would Jantid leave?"

Jade, nods agreeing, as she replies,

"I know Jim, and I have talked about it earlier, we would agree with you Janice, it spent at least a few years in the same spot, we doubt it would go anywhere, not until something big changed. Alright, so we know where we stand, I am wondering though, talking to Mr. Sage, he made mention of a small one..."

Janice's eyes widen, as Jade watches her confused. Janice grabs her head, as she answers shocked,

"Oh yeah, that's right! I had forgotten about that? I believe that was four or five years ago. We found a little one attached to a man who was swimming. This thing was maybe a foot-long at best. They believe the man died, I don't know what happened after that?"

Jade begins nodding, as she answers knowingly,

"Yes, that is the one Janice, he said they killed it, but what I am wondering now, is if Jantid is pregnant, and going to give birth, that may explain why it came into the shallow waters of Mexico? What if, it went back out to the middle of the ocean again? Leaving its young here? I know these are a lot of what ifs, but it's all I have to give right now?"

Janice looking at everyone's faces before worriedly stating,

"You don't think it's, oh my God."

Jade nods, as she responds,

"That is what I am thinking Janice. We haven't seen it for two days, if we don't see it today, we should start looking in the shallows for little ones, and if we find them, then we'll know one-hundred percent!"

Everyone tries talking all at once, Jade finally shouts,

"QUIET!"

Everyone stops talking, and stares at Jade, as she continues talking,

"I know we all want the same thing, Jantid dead. Why don't we start with looking in the swallows first, if nothing comes of that, then let's figure out the next step. Does this sound reasonable to everyone?"

Everyone nods agreeing, as Jade grins. Jim gets up and heads to the wheelhouse. Rick goes back to cleaning the equipment to prepare to deploy the sonar when they arrive to the swallows. Jade walks over to the bow, gripping the rails with both hands, as she looks at the blue water wondering. Shortly after, Janice makes her way towards Jade. Looking at Jade, her expression is blank, as she stares at the open sea. Janice taps Jade's arm lightly, as she asks,

"Are you alright Jade?"

Jade smiles, as she turns to look at Janice, noticing Janice let her hair down for the first time. Jade sighs, as she answers,

"Yeah, I'll be fine. Your black hair flows nicely against the blue of the water. Sorry, I just didn't notice how long your hair was before this?"

Janice snickers, as she responds,

"Thanks', I usually keep it up, easier than having a suspect grab a handful to help them escape. I'm really the one who should be shocked though… purple hair, I'm not sure the reasoning for that Jade?"

Jade looks out onto the water, laughing, as she answers,

"Honestly… something different. Plus, I wanted Mr. Sage to realize why I was trying to be late. He noticed that, even though I was early ha-ha!"

Janice starts laughing, as they continue chatting away. As the day goes on, a radio message crackles the radio to life,

"…The Cubin Military is on the beach conducting some sort of fire exercise, as reports of rapid gunfire is happening now…all boats are advised to stay clear of the area. As reports that are more accurate come in, we will keep all boaters informed. We will repeat this message every five minutes…this is the coastguard Tampa…

The message ends, as everyone looks at each other, and the decisions made to make a B-line for Cuba. An hour and twenty-three minutes later, the coastal line of Cuba appears. Seeing the gunfire through binoculars. A horn blows, a coastguard ship approaching on the port side. As the loudspeaker with a man's voice shouts,

"Attention Ship! It is not advised you proceed any further on your present course!"

Grabbing a megaphone, Jade responds,

"Coastguard, we are going to help them. If you look, they are firing at something further on the beach. We are assuming it is the creature we have been looking for."

The man looks towards the shore for a moment, then shouts,

"Okay, we will grant your request. We will follow behind, but if they fire at you…please return your ship to a safe distance. We will cover you if possible. Good Luck!"

Jade waves, and replies,

"Alright, and thank you coastguard!"

They continue towards the Cubin shore, the closer Jade, Janice, Rick, and Jim get, the more the creature becomes visible. The soldier's gunfire does not seem to be affecting it much. As everyone heads into the dingy after dropping the anchor. Heading to the shore, the gunfire is ear hurting, as the soldier's continuously shoot. Getting out of the dingy Jade runs up to one soldier, and whispers in his ear, he comes over to the dingy, and asks,

"What? You know what that thing is? Please tell us?"

Jade responds anxiously,

"A little bit, but we'll talk about that later, when did it come ashore?"

The army captain responds,

"I don't know, we were called by someone who said there was something killing people at Hahn's fish market. We got here and didn't see anything at first, not until it grabbed a private. That was about three hours ago."

Jade looks around at all the gunfire, and responds, as she points,

"Okay, if you keep trying to stop it from getting to the water, we will see what we can do to help you kill it, alright?"

The army captain answers confused, as he shoots at Jantid again,

"Okay? What can you do that bullets cannot?"

Jade responds hurriedly,

"Just keep it here! Let us handle that other part."

Jantid

The Captain begins shooting again. Jim, and Rick, head for the dingy, and head back to the ship. Another ship arrives this one has guns to spare. The soldiers begin to scatter, Jade and Janice run to the water's edge. The ship lights up like a 'Christmas tree', the sound of the massive guns ear shattering firing, as the building and beach begin exploding. The creature disappears into the sand and debris flying. The building collapses. After five minutes, the ship's guns silence, and the sand begins to settle, and the only thing moving is the smoke and fire in the remains of the building.

As the soldiers advance slowly on the debris, each step as if there was a mine in front of them. Watching them go through what remains of the building, piece-by-piece moving objects aside cautiously. They come to where the creature was last and begin moving objects even slower. A huge splash of water, the gunboat begins opening fire, as everyone hits the sand, turning to look. Jantid's tentacle(s) is wrapping around the gunboat, the coastguard begins firing at Jantid. Watching as Jantid flinches with every hit, but still manages to take the massive gunship down, as the coastguard begins moving away from Jantid.

Disappearing with ship in tow, only a couple of dozen people swimming for the shore. Screams coming a minute later as the almost transparent tentacles hit the surface of the water, slowly the two dozen men vanish under the water. A scream from the rubble, as a solider begins firing into a hole where a tentacle has him around the leg. As his comrades come to his aid, Jade and Janice know Rick and Jim are not coming back through the water in the dingy. Jade runs to the one soldier's truck, opening up the door, grabbing a fire extinguisher. Heading for the soldiers, Jade pulls the pin, and by the time she gets there, she is blasting the freezing foam around his leg. A moment later, the tentacle releases the soldier, and his friends carry him away. Still spraying towards the hole, Jade begins making her way back to the others. Once all together, one of the soldiers come towards Jade, and replies,

"Thank you for what you have done. What are these things anyways?"

Jade looks at him seriously, as she answers,

"You are welcome. I am not entirely sure, but I want to try and get this one alive, if possible?"

The army captain responds angrily,

"I don't think that is going to happen. We put thousands of bullets into it. Didn't have the effect we thought it would."

Jade nods as she looks around, and answers,

"I am sure you're right about that, but I have to try."

He bows his head, as he replies,

"You're braver then I am, I just want to kill it. What is it you need from me? If I have it, you can use it."

Jade looks at him, then his gun, and replies,

"Not really brave, you're the one with the guns. I just need to examine the creature. Perhaps I can kill that other one out there. Do you have any nitrogen? If you do we can perhaps freeze that thing, and maybe you will know how to deal with the next one if there are more than these two?"

The army captain looks thoughtful, as he looks towards a man in the distance, he shouts,

"I don't think we do? Hey Fernando, does that one facility have umm, nitrogen?"

Fernando shouts back, as he looks in the direction of the creature,

"Yes, Captain, I know they have nitrogen stored there."

He looks at Jade, as he hurriedly asks,

"How many do you think it will take to subdue this thing Ms.?"

Jade ponders for a quick second, as she answers,

"As many as you can muster, right now, I am working on a theory, nothing definite."

The army captain shouts,

"Okay, bring back as many as possible, and be 'quick', I don't want to be here after dark with these things out here."

Fernando responds loudly,

"Yes, Sir!"

The soldier grabs a few others to escort him to the facility, as the other soldiers watch the ocean and the debris of the building. Jim and Rick finally make their way back to the shore. The soldiers tell a story of pain, the ones looking at where the gunship had been, throw coins into the ocean, as a respectful gesture. Meanwhile, the waiting game continues…

#16

At the exact moment in Mexico, just a mere twelve miles away from Cancun, a group of men are meeting with Mr. Sage. Walking into a room, every footstep echoing. Coming to a stop in the center of the room with a single chair, Mr. Sage sitting down, and looking at the four shadowed men in front of him, as the tall one begins speaking,

(Russian accent) "Thank you for meeting with us Mr. Sage! As you know, we are willing to help get this blemish off our beautiful country. I assume you did as we asked?"

Mr. Sage nods agreeing, as he looks around wearily, and responds nervously,

"Yes, I told Jade, how to kill that thing like you said to. I also put that tracker on her boat, so you will know where she is at all times."

The man laughs, as he happily replies,

(Russian) "Good, good. Once we're rid of this abomination of our past, we can work on rebuilding Russia the way she used to be."

Mr. Sage treads lightly, as he asks,

Jantid

"Can I ask you gentlemen a question about this creature?"

The man glares angrily at him, as he responds,

(Russian accent) "Let me presume your question. You want to know what "it" is exactly."

Nodding slightly, Mr. Sage responds fearfully,

"Yes, I would like to know... please?"

They begin looking at each other, talking in Russian, and then nodding in agreement. The skinnier man steps forward, and replies,

"Okay Mr. Sage, I will tell you, but nothing leaves the confines of this room! Do I make myself clear as glass?"

Mr. Sage nods agreeing, as the man moves his suit jacket aside, revealing a holster as Mr. Sage replies,

"Oh... yes, you have my word as a gentleman."

The man slides his jacket over the holster, and nods, as he begins speaking,

"Very well Mr. Sage. As your word, I'll tell you. Back in nineteen eighty-six, a few months before the reactor had human faults that caused irrefutable destruction to our countries glory. We were sure, there was a spy who infiltrated the facility. The KGB had sent the best agents to Pripyat, a nearby town to Chernobyl. We believe this man caused the meltdown on April 26 of nineteen eighty-six. Therefore, once the alarms rang out, the agents had to turn to helping get the people out of the fire zone. On the other hand, as you know, it as the hot zone. During this time, the man escaped out of the country, making us look like incompetent fools."

The man stops to look around, and then continues talking,

"Twenty days after the meltdown, we sent in men to collect what we could, water samples, living animals, and such, trying to see, rather what effects the radiation had on them. Our scientists have found high levels of mutations in the aquatic animals. After these discoveries, we sent more people into the hot zone. They were trying to exterminate the entire animal population in there. The scientists in Moscow placed a squid, stingray, and Jellyfish in the same contaminated water. He wanted to see what changes would happen? What I heard was by the third generation, these three were one, and when he went to destroy it, apparently, it killed him. Everyone thought it was dead, but somehow it managed to live…"

He stops talking, as it sounds as if a vehicle stopped outside, one man goes to quickly check it out, and shakes his head. The man continues once the man at the door nods,

"A worker at the water plant stumbled across this creation, according to his co-worker. This thing was maybe six inches long, it shot a barb into the man's neck, killing him instantly. Another man nearby him said, after he fell dead, this creation slipped back into the water. The following months proved this creature was more than vicious, as little as it was. A trail of death in its path, as we were always at least one-step behind it. As it worked its way to the ocean, and we lost it, that is until it surfaced around here. Now we hope we can rid ourselves of this disgrace. Is this what you wanted to know, Mr. Sage?"

Mr. Sage nods, as he replies,

"…Yes, I did not need the whole story though, but yes."

The thin man glances at the others, and then looks straight at Mr. Sage holding his fist up while stating, as he individually raises three fingers,

"You see Mr. Sage. We believe that every story must have three things to make it interesting… depth to make sure you know it is real! A middle, so everything can sink in, and the most important part of all, this is the part where everything hits home…?"

Mr. Sage appears confused, as he looks at this man, and asks petrified,

"What is it, Sir?"

The man looks at the others for a moment shaking his index finger slightly, as he responds while turning to glance at Mr. Sage,

"I will tell you shortly, first I must ask you again, to make sure everything is in order. You told Jade everything we said to?"

Mr. Sage nods, and replies fearful,

"Yes, including the antimatter. I still do not understand that, why antimatter?"

The man grins, as he answers almost laughingly,

"Good. You know we are all friends here, so I will tell you. Antimatter is the most costly substance known to man, and we have plenty for sale. At the size of this creature, our government could afford to restart the weapons programs again."

Mr. Sage looks horrified, as he replies loudly,

"Dear God, you don't care if they kill it, you just want war…"

The man shakes his hand (No), as he responds sternly,

"No, we do not want war! Our people are jobless since we were unable to run these factories. This money would reopen them, and put people back to work."

Mr. Sage stares at him angrily, as he responds piercingly,

"I must warn Jade!"

The man looks irritated, as he replies calmly,

"Stop Mr. Sage… before you go telling anyone anything. Let me at least tell you what that third item is. Lastly, a story must have an ending…Goodbye Mr. Sage!"

Pulling his gun out, three shots ring out, as Mr. Sage falls lifelessly to the ground. The men walk by, and the last one fires a shot at point-blank range into his head. The last man grabs a jerry can and begins spewing gasoline all over the walls, including Mr. Sage's body. After a look around, he strikes a match and places it on the floor. A few seconds go by and a fire begins creeping towards Mr. Sage, and then the walls, soon the room becomes a fury of fire. The first man opens the door, and they all disappear as the door shuts behind them. Getting into a car, they drive off before anyone can see the burning building. The bulky man responds,

"Stupid man, he was told, do not ask questions, we paid him good money, now let's hope this woman Jade follows his advice."

The skinny man responds,

122

"I don't know Karlov, perhaps we should pay her a visit since we have the tracking device planted…give her a prompt, to ensure they buy from our government."

Karlov nods, as he responds,

"Perhaps you are right Nicholai, let's track her. Make a quick stop by her ship, before she leaves the dock."

Nicholai replies snarky,

"Yes, after all, we have the goods they need to kill this creature. Ha-ha!"

Karlov, snickers, as he replies laughing,

"You kill me, I don't think it will do much to it, after all, our government nuked it, and it still manages to live. I still remember the day they took out Chernobyl, and twenty thousand people to, nothing but a hole in the ground. I doubt antimatter is going to have any effect on it?"

Nicholai responds curiously,

"You were there when they found the creature boss?"

Karlov nods, as he sighs, then answers,

"Yes! I was younger, a soldier of mother Russia, a great honor of the time. I was stationed in Chernobyl at that time. The orders came from the top scientists, this creation of theirs was loose in the country. We were told, don't approach it, and that it was no bigger than a hand. Seems, this creation managed to find its way into the plant. After three dozen people died, knowing there was no possible way to explain so many deaths away. They told us under strict orders, we were to blow the reactors. Hoping to destroy this creature, we set in motion, the events leading up to April 26, 1986 at 1:23 A.M. A day that will forever chill me until my dying breath. That is why it is imperative that we rebuild Russia to her former glory. Once we can do that, our people will live in peace, while these people suffer the pain we all have."

Nicholai looks somber, as he replies,

"Yes, I can't believe you had to endure that pain, but you are right, it's their problem now! Let them figure it out, of course after they pay. Ha-ha!"

Karlov answers while lighting a cigar,

"Yes, they will be looking quite surprised to find that does nothing to it…Ha-ha-ha! You know Nicholai… speaking about the old times brings back thoughts about this one man… Alex Travois. Months after the meltdown happened, intelligence was brought to our attention. A secret operative group was in the hot zone. Right under our noses too! Orders came down from the top, get them out of there! That's just what we did Nicholai."

Nicholai grins, as he answers,

"I wish I were there with you. What did you do to this man Alex Travois?"

Karlov takes a puff from his cigar, then answers delightedly,

"Yes, a proud moment indeed. We readied ourselves for a fight. When we found their truck, it was huge, how could we have missed it for that long? This vehicle was two stories high, and as long as two, maybe three tanks. Anyways… we open fired on this truck, killing the one driving, and ten men and women along with them. This Travois,

124

he must have been the leader, as he was dressed in an army uniform. We took him to KGB headquarters…"

Nicholai grins even more, as he asks excitedly,

"KGB headquarters? Oh, he must have cried for his mommy being there?"

Karlov laughs, as he pats Nicholai while he starts talking,

"Not really. Although, he did beg for his life near the end. I was there when they interrogated Mr. Travois. The agent asked him many questions, the one question I ponder the most, the one of why there were only twelve people, and fourteen beds? Oh well, some questions aren't meant to be answered. Travois died some seven months later, he never gave anything up, too bad. He may have provided some useful information."

#17

As the sun begins to set over Cuba, the soldiers still poised to shoot anything that moves un-expectantly. An old truck drives up onto the beach, they have returned with the Nitrogen. As they begin to unload the tanks off the truck onto the sand. Everyone hurriedly turns as they begin hearing sounds coming from the debris. As a few soldiers run to take aim at what might be coming out, the others try to unload the eight more tanks left on the truck. After setting the last one down, they turn, and wait for what Jade wants them to do next?

After talking to Jade, she gets the soldiers to move two of the larger Nitrogen cylinders close to the building debris, confused, but they do it. As the sunset begins casting the shadow of darkness all around. Armed with a few lights, and a beach fire to emanate a wider glowing light. An hour after the sun has completely left the sky. A sound of rubble shifting around catches everyone's attention. Guns clicking, and lights pointing towards the bomb out building, a light catches one of the monster's tentacles, as it emerges from where it had grabbed that last soldier. A gurgling sound echoes while making its way back towards the water.

As it creeps closer to the one Nitrogen cylinder, Jade leans into the Captain, and whispers in his ear,

"I want you to fire at that tank, try to hit it near Jantid. This way, the explosion will impact him directly."

The Captain nods, as he gives a hand signal, within ten seconds, four shots ring out, followed what can only, be described as a sonic boom. A loud demented howl of pain rings out, near the (boom) as the explosive light subsides, and in the darkening light, lays Jantid, covered in liquid Nitrogen. As stone cold as can be. The creature leaning up against the second Nitrogen cylinder, which is still spewing out nitrogen. Driving an army truck nearby, with a spotlight focused on the frozen creature. Splashing sounds coming from the ocean, like a whale breaching the water.

Ten soldiers watch the ocean, as the other soldiers creep up on the monster frozen in front of them. One soldier yells angrily,

"YOU'RE NOT GOING TO KILL ANYONE ELSE!"

Before Jade, Janice, or the Captain can get over there to stop them, the soldiers begin smashing the creature into hundreds of pieces. The Captain quickly fires a single shot into the air. The damages done, Jade, Rick, and Jim are left to collect the remains piece by piece. Placing them into containers, as Janice tries to find more containers. The Captain disciplines his men for this, but they continue to watch the ocean for another visitor. The night is long, and quiet, as the Captain comes over to Jade, and starts talking to her,

"I am sorry for my men earlier. I know you wanted that so you could inspect it. They did not understand this, they assumed it was going to come back alive. One of my men told me, a couple of local anglers brought this thing in yesterday morning. He said the owner Hahn, froze this creature, he removed it this morning and threw it out. This thing came back alive after a whole day in the freezer…"

Jade looks disappointed, but holds it in, as she replies,

"Yes, I understand why they would shoot it, Captain. I just wish they had not done it to this one. One thing I have learned from this experience, Nitrogen will have an ill effect on it. I am sorry about the loss of your men Captain."

He nods while glancing back towards the beach, and responds sympathetically,

"Thank you. In the morning, we will help you put these containers on your ship. I will leave you to your work now and thank you for your help. We appreciated it, even though you didn't have to. Again, I apologize for destroying your specimen. "

The army captain stands there still worriedly looking around, as Jade answers,

"You're welcome. I'm glad we were close enough to help out. I will see you in the morning Captain."

The Captain heads back to his men, peeking back at Jade every so often. As the stars twinkle brightly in the moonlight, the waves swoosh on the shore. The night tiptoes on, everyone sleeps soundly except the ones patrolling the parameters.

At first dawn, everyone begins moving the containers to the dingy, the smell wafting from the dead creature, overwhelming the senses of the one's carrying these containers. Finally, Jade and her crew are on their way back to Mexico, the sonar bleeping away, as something big follows behind them.

#18

A submarine the U.S.S Great white, on a routine patrol between Mexico, and Cuba. The radar begins picking up a slight disturbance in front of the sub. A thud sends everyone lurching forward quickly. As Captain Morris, gets his bearing about him, he shouts,

"Get me the surface!"

Radioman, Jack Burns, tries to message the surface repeatedly,

"Sir. The radio is out."

Captain Morris looks angry, as he walks over to the radio, grabbing the headset away from Jack, as he flicks various switches. Throwing the headset down on the console, as he states puzzled,

"Alright men… we are currently unable to reach the surface for guidance. You all continue to try and get us out of whatever has us stuck? I'm going to address the men."

Flicking the intercom switch, Captain Morris wipes his brow, as he clears his throat, and states,

"Attention crew of the U.S.S. Great White. This is Captain Dale Morris, we have encountered a situation. One that hopefully will be cleared up quickly. We cannot reach the surface via communications. That is all!"

Flicking the switch again, Captain Morris shifts his eyes to each of the officers on deck while sweat begins to cascade down his face. Walking over to his chair, he collapses, as he eyes the instrument panels shaking his head unknowingly. Fourteen-minutes pass before he sits forward, and asks demandingly,

"Do we have any idea what is happening yet, anyone?"

Everyone just turns and stares blankly, as he glares at them. Standing up angrily, he responds loudly,

"I want to meet with all the officers in the briefing room immediately!"

Captain Dale Morris is at wits end, trying to figure out what they're caught on? Everyone rushes to the briefing room. After two hours of discussing what's going on outside his submarine, he is no closer to figuring out any of the five "W's". Captain Dale removes his hat frustrated, standing up, and stating with distress,

"I'm worried about the subs twelve-degree tilt to the right, and I'm sure we can agree, we haven't hit anything, what does that tell you?"

Engineer Robert's responds questioningly,

"Sir, that tells me, we would be either out of water, or we hit something soft enough not to be detected by our instruments…"

Jantid

Captain Dale Morris, stares at the subs blueprints, walking over to them, as he points and responds curiously,

"Yes, I have thought about that Engineer Roberts. Our problems, we're tilted, our propellers are dragging heavily. This tells me we are in, or on something dense. We could send someone out, but we are in a depth of twelve hundred and eighteen feet. If we are wrong and open up the emergency release, we could all die! If we are in something dense, it could crush the hull? Do we dare send someone out there?"

First officer Gerald looks worried, as he nervously replies,

"Captain! May I make a suggestion?"

Captain Morris acknowledges him while turning to look, as he responds curiously,

"Go ahead, Gerald? Let's hear it?"

Gerald taps the table, as he nervously answers,

"Well, I know this is untried, but perhaps instead of opening the main hatch, what if we open torpedo tube two, in full diving gear. I should be able to fit inside, if someone hits fire, the outer tube will open for three seconds. That should be enough time to find out if we are in water or jammed up against something else?"

Captain Morris grimaces, as he ponders, and then looks straight at Gerald, and asks inquisitively,

"Are you sure you want to volunteer for this? You know we won't be able to save you if you get sucked out by the pressure."

Gerald stands up, and replies semi-confidently,

"Yes, I am Sir! I understand everything I have suggested, I have thought about the outcome even before I suggested it…Sir!"

Captain Morris nods approvingly, and replies concerned,

"Very well, we will try this. Hopefully, we will get an answer to our problem here, good luck to you Gerald."

Gerald salutes, as he replies loudly,

"Yes, thank you, Sir! I will be ready in five minutes!"

Saluting again, as he walks past the Captain, the rest stay sitting there straight-faced, but happy it is not one of them. They begin dispersing back to their stations, as the Captain sits down and taps his hat on the table. Realizing he may have just sent a man to his death if anything goes wrong. The loudspeaker crackles to life.

"Captain to the bridge!"

Standing up, and heading to the bridge, a heaviness on his face, as he arrives to take control. Officer O'Neal nods, Dale walks over to him, and whispers,

"Everything is a go?"

O'Neal looks at the Captain sternly, as he answers solemnly,

"Yes Captain, everything is ready on your command."

Captain Dale stands tall, as he sighs a heavy breath before responding unsure,

"Thank you. Ready to fire tube two! On my mark, three, two, one…now."

Officer O'Neal pushes the fire button. Waiting on pins and needles, the red firelight comes on and stays lit for four seconds then turns off. As the Captain nervously waits for word of what happened, or if Gerald is gone? The look on his face becomes that of a broken wreck of a man, as the time tick's away. Finally, a man comes running up to the Captain shouting,

"He made it Captain!"

A smile breaks across his face once again, as they run to meet up with Gerald. Once they reach his cabin, they rush in. He finishes taking off his wetsuit, and looks at the Captain, and responds seriously,

"Sir, we are caught in some sort of gel, there is breathable air out there, its heavy air, but breathable. I did not see much in that short time, but I would like to go out and check it out further Captain?"

Captain Morris, looks astonished, as he ponders sending him out again. Looking at the others around before asking,

"Are you positive that is breathable? Not that you were breathing the air from within the sub?"

Gerald looks thoughtful, then replies,

"Yes, Sir! I took in a big gulp of air, it may be a little stale and heavy, but it should be breathable long enough for us to find out what's going on exactly, sir."

The captain ponders, as he looks at his first officer for any resistance. Receiving nothing, he replies,

"Okay, your discovery, take a gun with you, just in case, permission granted. Also, see if you can fix our communications as well if you are able to find the problem?"

Gerald stands up, and salutes while he replies,

"Yes, Sir! I will, thank you, Sir!"

As everyone anxiously readies for the hatch to open, most are weary and wearing oxygen masks, but as it opens and the air decompresses, everyone gives a big breath of relief. Taking the masks off, smiling. Gerald climbs outside first and stands there for a moment before saying anything. He yells down,

"Sir, I would suggest taking a look at this…a world of its own, like we went from the deep blue sea to a pinkish white world. The antenna is gone Sir, probably when we crash into this place. There is a little bit of water coming in from where we came in Sir. If the water keeps coming like this we should be able to reverse out in a couple of hours, maybe more Captain?"

Captain Dale Morris listens closely before answering,

"Great! I am coming up next."

As the Captain climbs up, the others follow him until they are all standing outside of the sub. Gerald responds cautiously,

"I am going to check around the base of the sub Captain."

The captain nods approvingly, and replies,

"Alright, Gerald. Be careful, we have no idea what may be in here with us?"

Walking away towards the front of the sub, looking on what the sub is sitting on, climbing down, he sinks in about six inches. Trudging around, looking for a sign of something, anything that explains what this place is? Sloshing around in the water that is rising slowly, catching a glimpse of something under the murkiness of the water. Kneeling down trying to grab it. Catching it in his hand, looking at this weirdly shaped creature, about one inch long and almost transparent. Gerald shouts out,

"Ouch!"

Grabbing the back of his leg, the one on his hand latches on. Soon his screams of pain echo loud enough to catch everyone's attention. Watching from the top of the sub as Gerald falls into the water covered in these micro creatures, within a minute the water turns a reddish color. Soon a stream of these little things head towards the submarine. The Captain, unable to see Gerald, calls out,

"Gerald, what's happening? Come back here NOW!"

With no answer coming back, nine men head for the front of the sub. Looking around frightened, using binoculars, and not seeing a trace of anything? The men start making their way back into the sub. The little line of thousands of these creatures making their way up to where the men were standing. Soon the micro creatures make their way towards the open hatch.

Leaving the hatch open until the Captain is certain, Gerald isn't coming back. Hurriedly ordering the hatch closed. The last man in grabs the hatch, and begins to close it when something lands on his face. Falling down onto the metal floor, knocking himself unconscious. No one realizing he didn't close the hatch.

A passing sailor sees him lying on the floor, hiking the unconscious man over his shoulder he carries him to the doctor, who is nearby checking on another man's minor injury. He places the unconscious man on a table. The doctor comes walking over quickly, grabbing his penlight. Looking into the man's eyes, then quickly checking the man's neck. Shaking his head no, as he responds saddened,

"This man is dead. Where did you find Anthony?"

The man stares at the dead man, and exclaims,

"He was by the hatch we came in."

The doctor nods, as he begins checking for broken bones while answering,

"I'm figuring he broke something when he fell? He doesn't seem to have anything broken, just a bump on his head. Wait? What is this on his face?"

The doctor begins trying to remove whatever's attached to the sailors face. Grabbing a set of tweezers, and pulling, as Anthony's cheek moves with whatever this is. That's when the doctor realizes it is or was biting him. Calling for the Captain, when he arrives they both look at the mess, and the Captain shouts loudly,

"Damn it! This has to be that creatures young! Looks like a goddamned squid. Where the hell did you find this man sailor?"

Seaman Blaine gulps, as Captain Morris gets in his face. The frightened man responds quickly,

"I found him at the hatch, sir!"

The captain grimaces, while losing himself in thought. Glancing down at the dead man, as he exclaims,

"Damn… we must have penetrated a birth sack or the creature itself? Either way, we have to destroy this creature or its babies at all costs."

All the sailors, including the doctor, have stunned expressions on their faces. The doctor walks up to the Captain, and asks concerned,

"Are you absolutely positive Captain? Is it possible this is a one-off?"

The captain firmly shakes his head, as he looks at everyone before responding,

"I would, and am going to bet my life on it. Before we left port, my commander filled me in that this creature moved into the waters near Mexico…"

Before the Captain can say another word, alarms begin ringing, red lights pulsating. Everyone looks around, waiting for a message to come over the intercom. A man comes running in and stops short of hitting the Captain yelling frantically.

"Sir, there are foreign creatures on board. They're crawling in through the open hatch, we have it closed now, but these things are attacking the men all over the ship!"

The captain screams angrily,

"They are inside…kill them, capture them, but get them the hell off this sub!"

The man responds while screaming echoes throughout the corridors,

"Yes, Sir!"

The sailor runs out of the room, screaming heard coming from multiple places. Finally, another man comes running towards the doctor, falling down. Three creatures attached to his face and neck."

The captain stares at the man writhing on the floor in pain. He grimaces, while he shouts,

"Doctor, if we don't stop them here and now, they're going to overtake the ship. I must order the destruction of this submarine."

The doctor fearfully responds,

"You cannot do that Captain, the men will kill them. Give them some time."

The captain looks at him angrily, and responds with confidence,

"I cannot take that chance doctor. If these things live, nothing in the seas or oceans will be the same again."

The doctor replies disheartened,

"Yes, Sir! Could you not give them a little longer though?"

The captain shouts as he points down the hall towards the screams,

"Listen to them scream, doctor! Those screams coming from the men are getting to be more, not less. We can't wait any longer, it will only be a matter of moments before we are doomed."

Jantid

The Captain runs for the control room, jumping over men laying on the ground wreathing in pain, some already dead. Finally, getting to the self-destruct panel, opening it up, and begins a sequence of numbers and letters. A pained look comes on his face, as he slams his right leg hard. Thirty seconds after, all the lights flicker green, then turn yellow. A loudspeaker comes to life.

"You have five minutes to abandon the U.S.S. Great white, or press the stop sequence to abort!"

The Captain looks at his hand, another little creature begins biting him, as he slams his hand against the periscope. Killing the thing and pulling it off, but not before another, then another. Soon the Captains screams mixes in with the others. The doctor comes running to the Captains aid. Kneeling down, pulling the creatures off one by one and collecting a few on himself. The doctor begins screaming, pulling one off his calf. Captain Morris grabs the doctor's arm, as he fights the pain, and whispers with clinched teeth,

"I, I had no choice, God forgive me. I had to…"

The Captain's eyes fix and dilate, as he slumps over. The doctor's screams get louder as more attach to him. Everyone's screams echo throughout the sub, drowning out the alarms going off. As the counter counts down the minutes, one-minute-forty-two seconds. The only sounds heard, are that of the alarm and the timer counting down.

#19

Watching as the large object comes to a dead stop, Jade, and the others all huddle around the monitor. Everyone's eyes just watch, as the beeps become slower and slower until they stop completely. Jade begins looking back for any signs of anything on the surface that may be disrupting their signal. Nothing? Rick turns towards Jade, and asks,

"Could it possibly be a sub? After all, it's at a depth of at least 1200 feet."

Jade turns around, and states thoughtfully,

"Yes, but submarines don't vanish off radars just like that. No, something's wrong about this, and I don't like one bit."

Janice walks over to Jade, and replies calmly,

"I've never scuba dived out this far, but what if it went under a rock ledge? Is that possible for a sub to do?"

Jade seemingly thinks about this for a moment, then smiles, as she answers a little less stressed,

"That's could be possible Janice."

Jantid

As the stench worsens from the many pieces of creature everyone heads inside the wheelhouse, in hopes of escaping the putrid smell. Getting little relief, but barely, looking through the binoculars, and seeing Mexico appearing slowly, Jade turns to Jim, and responds,

"Can you not get this boat moving faster?"

Jim nods, as he grabs the throttle, and pushes them forward another notch, and responds cautiously,

"I will try, but we are already pushing it into the red zone."

An hour and change go by and finally, Mexico is right there, a mile away. An almost sonic boom causes Jade and the rest of them quickly turning towards the stern. Watching a huge gush of water, shooting a hundred feet into the sky. Grabbing the binoculars, Jade looks back towards Cuba. Seeing water splashing back down, maybe fifteen miles from Cuba. Jade responds startled,

"I wonder what the hell that explosion was about? Could that have been that gunboat?"

Janice gazes at the mist that is falling from the sky, as she replies thoughtfully,

"Was that not the area where that thing quit following us?"

Jade looks intrigued, as she tries to consider the distance. She nods agreeing slightly, and responds,

"I believe you are right Janice, I think that may have been a submarine, possibly a nuclear one at that?"

As the smoke rises from the water in the distance, the coastguard head back towards Cuba, as Jade and the others continue to Cancun. After reaching the dock, detective Frank Jorden is waiting until the boats tied down. He has a handful of files under his arm, as he grabs the bow rope. Jim and Rick are the first off, bandannas across their faces. Frank begins to ask, as the smell wafts across his nose,

"What's with the…? Oh Dear God"… (Heaving)… "What the hell is that…?"(Leaning over the edge of the dock, and vomiting)

Janice, pats Frank on the back, as Jade, Rick, and Jim carry the rotting carcass to coolers and sealing them up. After a good twenty minutes, Frank finally drops his last bit of lunch. Following them to the police labs, they place the coolers into a freezer and clean up from the last twenty-four hours. After an hour, Frank begins banging on doors trying to get everyone where he can talk with them. Soon he tells them to meet him in the conference room as soon as possible. Waiting once again, he finds himself on his second cup of coffee by the time Janice makes her way into the room. Eventually, the rest come in slowly, and relaxed, Frank begins telling them what's been happening, as he states annoyed,

"Well thank you all for joining me 'finally!' First, I would like to express my disappointment in you all. I understand your commitment to finding this creature, monster, or whatever it is. You Jade, I got a call from the minister in charge of foreign affairs. Do you know what he told me? I am sure you do, but let me tell you what he told me. He said, he sent Mr. Sage to help us determine the best course of action. You told him he was not allowed on your boat…I asked myself this question too, now I am going to ask you…why…?"

Jade looks at his angry face, as she leans forward, and responds irritated,

"Well if you must know. I am funded by private sources, those conditions they impose declare, 'no government personnel' on the boat, and he was allowed to come aboard when I changed boats, not before!"

Frank Jordan looks confused, as he tries to figure out Jade's answer. He finally asks,

"What is so important that no government personal are allowed on your boat?"

Jade stares at Frank hard. As everyone watches her closely, she responds angrier,

"I have delicate equipment on board, one miss calibration, and it would cost hundreds of thousands to fix. Perhaps you are unaware, but government people do not leave things alone, so he had to wait a day, so what?"

Detective Jordan grimaces, as he leans down, and replies sternly,

"He is dead! We tried to get ahold of you, no answer on your boat."

Jade looks sorrowful, as she answers,

"I am sorry he died, but the four of us have been out on the ocean trying to get rid of Jantid! Perhaps that smell you whiffed before barfing was a clue to what we had been up to for the last twenty-four hours?"

Frank looks shocked, and excited, as he responds hopeful,

"What…? You got that creature?"

Jade stares at him shaking her head no, and replies,

"No, we got what is possibly a baby of this creature. The big one is still out there, but we are getting closer to understanding how to kill it."

Frank looks shocked, turning pale as memories of that smell kick in. Once he gets ahold of himself again, he answers,

"So that is a baby? God they smell awful. Anyways before I forget. Jade, so did you let Mr. Sage on the boat?"

Jade sits forward, and responds sternly,

"Yes, the next day around noon. The day before, we heard an explosion and went to offer help, looks like two boats collided, by the time we got there, nothing but debris floating there."

Detective Frank nods, as he continues to try to shake off that sickly sensation, as he responds,

"Yes, we found out more about that. Apparently, three men chartered a boat. They picked up depth charges as well. I can only assume this…they were more than likely monster hunting, the Oldman who sold the depth charges said, his friend Devon, a skilled Captain had reservations about letting them on board, but he did. We think they may have thrown one depth charge out, causing the other boat to swerve to miss it, and accidentally hit them instead. All I know is two boats went down, but we cannot send anyone down safely. Until we take care of this monstrosity that has taken our waters over."

Jade nods agreeing, as she answers,

144

Jantid

"That would explain it. We just heard an explosion, which reminds me? We believe a sub blew up just off the coast of Cuba."

Frank looks shocked, as he responds concerned,

"What? A Sub? You mean the military kind?"

Jade stands up, walking over to a map, and points to where, as she responds,

"Yes, it was following us then stopped. Maybe, an hour later, a huge explosion."

Frank looks at Jade seriously, and questioningly asks,

"Wow. What do you think happened out there?"

Jade returns to her chair, looking hard at detective Jorden, and replies sternly,

"My guess would be Jantid, but that is speculation on my part. I have to ask, were you offering a reward to anyone who killed Jantid?"

Frank shakes his head no, as he quickly replies,

"No, the night before we were warning people what to look for, and if possible stay away from the ocean. My guess, residents who wanted to get rid of it quick. We are still waiting to hear who these men are?"

Jade looks around teary-eyed, sorrowfully responding,

"Oh I see, I am sorry if we caused you any grief, I am pretty set in my ways when it comes to this monster. Three years I have spent trying to kill it. Now I learn it can have babies too. We will get it, I feel confident about that."

Frank calmly responds,

"Yes, I can understand your point, Jade. Once this creature is dead, we can all enjoy life again. I will tell the minister you had nothing to do with Mr. Sage's death."

Jade looks down at the table for a moment, as she responds curiously,

"Thank you, I will also say Mr. Sage planted a bug on my boat, I am not sure why? I placed in the tire, this way they would think we never left."

Frank looks extremely confused, as he hesitates before asking,

"A bug, why? Do you have something super-secret on board your boat?"

Jade nods, glancing around. Looking Mr. Jorden in the eyes, and whispering,

"I do, that is why no one of government nature is allowed on board. That is why I have two boats with the same name. These devices could be converted to weapon status in a matter of moments."

Frank is taken aback, as he sits down slowly while responding quietly,

"Holy, are you military Jade?"

Jade looks at Frank coldly, as she replies,

"No, I am just a Marine biologist, but I am not a normal Biologist, I work exclusively with animals who have been mutated by radiation.

I have no affiliation with any government. That allows me to access different countries without hassle."

Frank slowly nods, as he puts pieces together, and responds,

"I guess that is why the U.S. government could not find you as a resident."

Jade nods, and replies,

"Yes, I have passports to every country, but no actual citizenship anywhere. I am sure you have more pressing things to do, then ask me a bunch of questions about me detective?"

Frank turns to Janice, and looks saddened, as he replies,

"Yes, this is the sad part for me. Janice, I tried to fight for you, but the chief has fired you, for neglecting your duties. I can only say I am sorry."

Janice looks shocked, and stunned, as she replies,

"What? Fired me for what? Helping out Jade, you asked me to. Why would they fire me?"

Frank looks at Janice, holding his hands up while trying to calm her down, as he states,

"I am sorry Janice. They said, many of your reports were not right, and if I covered for you, then I would be fired as well. I did my best, I promise you, I did."

Janice stands up angrily, and shouts,

"Bullshit Frank, you saved your own skin and left me to rot. I will clean out my desk right now!"

Jade looks at Frank with distaste, as she replies harshly,

"That is low Frank! You are a genuine piece of work."

Standing up, everyone glares at Frank, shaking his or her heads, following Janice to her desk. Jade, helps Janice pack, and Jim and Rick carry the boxes to the boat. The other officer's watch confused, as the four leave.

Heading back to the boat. Rick and Jim quickly put the boxes down, and leave. Janice and Jade sit down on the bench near the bow. Jade looks at Janice's tears running down her face, a saddened dishearten look. Jade reaches over, puts a hand softly on her shoulder, and responds quietly,

"Janice, you are welcome to come with us, paid of course. We can use the help, besides it's nice to have another woman to talk with."

Janice's jaw lowers twitching, as she responds,

"…What? I don't have the skills you are looking for though?"

Jade smiles, as she grabs Janice's hand, and replies,

"That is where you are wrong Janice, you are exactly who we are looking for, you don't have papers, but you do have the exact skills we need to help stop Jantid. Don't sell yourself short like that."

Rick comes back up the plank with a tray holding four coffee's, as Jade's talking. Walking up to Janice, stopping near them both. Handing Jade a coffee, then Janice, as he responds,

"I overheard what Jade said, and Jade is right. You have never been asked to leave the boat by Jade. That is a skill only two others have, Jim, and I. Besides, I've never seen Jade so happy."

Jantid

Janice looks up at Rick, smiling, as she responds,

"Thank you, Rick. Okay, if you are sure, then I'll accept."

Janice turns to look at Jade, as Jim smiles, and replies happily,

"Great! Welcome to our family! Let's get you unpacked."

#20

On the bright morning of August 2, at the police station. Jade, Janice, and Rick rummage through the last of the pieces of what could be Jantid's offspring? Unsure, as they pick pieces up with tweezers, placing them on trays. Detective Jorden watches Janice from the observation window. Jade walks over to Janice, holding a small tray with little pieces of teeth. Putting the tray down beside Janice, as Jade responds,

"I believe we have all the teeth we're going to find. There are some full teeth in there. If you can make somewhat of a line of teeth. Try to go biggest to smallest. Hopefully, we'll be able to get an insight into its mouth."

Janice nods while sliding the tray in front of herself. Glancing at Jade, with a smile, as she answers,

"I'll do my best Jade. Thank you for letting me help you."

Jade pats Janice on the back, and replies,

"Thank you! I know you will."

Hours trickle along, as the trio start to piece the shattered beast together again. Finally, Janice calls over to Jade, Rick,

"Guys, I think I have the teeth together, as good as they're going to get."

Jade and Rick rush over, as Jade responds,

"Damn! You even managed to put the broken ones together, sweet."

Jade, Janice, and Rick spend a good hour checking over the teeth. Jade finally shakes her head in amazement while stating,

"These are the teeth of a highly evolved eating system, which allows them to eat while they hunt, and dissolve their prey in record time, perhaps three to five minutes. Much like the spider, turning its victim into liquid. The first ten rows of teeth have special glands that discharge enzymes that breakdown everything from skin to metals into their smallest components. These enable the next twenty sets of teeth to absorb the nutrient-rich liquids in a timely manner, much like drinking through a straw. The rest of the teeth seem to be a disposal system, they may or may not keep these nutrients stored? I doubt we'll be able to piece this section together properly. Not seeing an original one, we'd be just guessing?"

Janice and Rick stand there with their mouths opened, not knowing what to say. Jade continues looking at the teeth for a moment, as she responds,

"Come with me over here, and I'll show you what I've pieced together."

They all head over to where Jade is working, as she points at the tentacles, as she states,

"See these transparent tentacles, they are much like a man of wars. They cause extreme pain and inhibit the ability to move properly. As for the darker tentacles, these are that of a squid, they plunge these hooks to ensure whatever it grabs does not go anywhere. There was a strange barb, unsure if it belongs to the creature or a stingray it ate, but at the very back of what would be its mouth, approximately six inches long and sharp. The DNA suggests that squid, Jellyfish, and then stingray, squid being the supreme DNA count. Finding a weakness in the chain of this one anyway, could prove to be difficult? We know what Nitrogen does to it, but that's out of water."

Rick responds,

"Three creatures in one? Each would have their own immunity problems, wouldn't they Jade?"

Jade ponders for a moment, as Janice responds,

"They're all sea creatures, what about regular water?"

Jade, and Rick, glance over at Janice grinning, as Jade answers,

"You know, we can try that. I have nothing else right now that wouldn't endanger a multiple species of wildlife. Let's go grab a bunch of regular waters and check this out. Worst case scenario, we have lots of drinking water."

Getting as many bottles of water as can be mustered, they make their way to the boat, after loading the water on, a couple of men wearing dark suits make their way to Jade's boat, and stop, looking at Jade, the one man is husky unshaven, and has been drinking. The man yells to Jade,

(Russian accent) "YOU THERE!"

Jade looks at the man irritated, and shouts back,

"What?"

The man walks onto the boat, and over to Jade, and whispers,

(Russian accent) "We know how to kill the beast you search for."

Jade looks puzzled, as the man nods while she glances at him, and responds inquisitively,

"Who are you guys anyways?"

The man answers,

"I am Koslov I am a man who has searched for this creature for years. You need antimatter to kill it."

Jade looks at this man suspiciously, as she replies,

"Really? Do you know what that costs? Geez everyone in the world would be bankrupt."

Koslov responds humbly,

"Yes, but that creature would be dead. After all, is that not what we all want?"

Jade shakes her head disgusted, and replies,

"Yes, but I could never get my hands on that kind of money. We're in two different ballparks."

Koslov nods, as he casually answers,

"I may be able to broker a deal between sellers, and buyers…"

Jade still looks at him with untrusting eyes, as she replies,

"Fine, you talk to everyone you need to, contact them, and see what you get for a response. We have to go now, thank you for the information."

Koslov stands there puzzled, as he responds,

"…But…but…"

Jim ushers Kaslov off the boat, as the two men look bewildered. Watching as the boat revs up and backs away from the pier, the two men stand there puzzled by their leaving without finding out anything of what they were talking about, and one man turns to the other and responds.

"Do you think they have found a way to kill it?"

Koslov responds angrily,

"I hope not, we need that money back in Russia, we have that tracker on the boat, we can always find them later."

The other man responds,

"Yes, perhaps we should go rent a boat, and follow them out…"

As the two men try to figure out where the boat rentals are, Jade gets further out of sight. On the boat, Jade is talking with Janice,

"Those two men back at the dock. Those are a prime example of people up to something. Scammers if you will, the antimatter they were speaking of, that is expensive. I am talking billions of dollars."

Janice looks worried, as she asks,

"How often do men like that come around?"

Jade's cheeks puff up, as she responds,

"Anytime they think there is a goldmine to be had, the problem is, they are dangerous too. I am thinking they were the ones that sent Mr. Sage to see me, to butter me up. Since he is dead, I am sure they killed him because he did not do what he was supposed to do. I am sure we will see them again, just keep their faces in mind."

Janice nods, as she answers,

"Yes, I will keep my eyes peeled for people like that in the future."

As the two friends chat, a sonar blip catches the attention of Rick, who looks to see what is happening. The blips turn into beeps then a constant hum. Jade comes running in, followed by Janice, and Jim. The four of them stare, as the now two objects appear to be heading towards each other at a depth of three hundred feet. Jim looks towards the direction of one. Janice looks in the direction of the other. Looking over the side, into the clear abyss. Jade responds,

"Let's drop a camera in and see what is happening down there, they are only a hundred feet apart."

Jim heads to the stern, grabbing the metal case, opening it up. Attaching cables to the camera and turning it on. Standing up, holding the camera over the side, and beginning to lower it into the water. Jim nods to Jade, who turns the monitor on. The picture starts to focus and flickers, and down in the barely lit darkness is two Jantid's. Their shadowed outlines unforgettable. Jade looks shocked, shaking her head, as she responds,

"Okay, keep on this course Rick. I do not want to be on top of them if they come up to the surface."

Rick looks at the controls, and responds,

"Yes Jade, I will speed up three knots."

Jade nods, as she watches the Jantid's slowly making their way towards each other. She replies,

"Thank you, Rick."

Rick clicks the throttle three times, as everyone else watches the monitor. The two creatures entangle themselves in what looks like a death lock. As everyone's eyes are piercing the screen, watching what could be a Godsend of miracles happening before their eyes. Janice looks up when she hears a beeping sound in the distance, grabbing the binoculars, and seeing those two men from earlier coming in another boat. Janice taps Jade on the shoulder, breaking her concentration on what is happening below. Janice replies,

"Jade, look, we have company!"

Jade looks to where Janice is pointing. Jade looks angry, as she replies,

"What the heck! Are they crazy, Rick, move us away from here, these asses are going get themselves killed if those Jantid's realize there is a boat above."

Rick looks back shaking his head, as he answers,

"Right away!"

The boat speeds up, Jim is watching the events unfold below, and shouts,

"Too late Jade, they are making their way to the surface."

Jade turns to Jim quickly, and yells,

"What? Oh no. Let me see."

Jade looks into the monitor, seeing the Jantid's no longer locked together, but are rising to the surface, seeing the transparent tentacles in the monitor. Looking towards the stern, the other boat is above where they are. Jim is waving them to go another way, all they do is wave back and keep coming. Jade comes running onto the deck in time to see the transparent tentacles sitting on the surface, around the other boat. Soon eight tentacles, dark ones begin feeling the other boat. Hearing screams coming from the other boat, and soon gunfire. As the situation escalates, and the two Jantid's have the boat sitting in the goo that is them. Watching as they hopelessly fight a losing battle, Janice replies,

"Should we try and help them?"

Jade shakes her head, as she responds,

"No, even if we did, we would all be dead. Especially against two of them."

Janice looks at them fearfully, as she replies,

"Yeah, I guess, I just wish there was something we could do."

Jade grabs Janice's arms, and looks her dead in the eyes, as she replies,

"You did Janice when you saw them, you told us, and we tried to get them to change their heading. That is what makes this work humbling, so many times all you can do is sit back and watch. Occasionally you can save them, but that is far and few between. Do not burden yourself with this. You will come to see what I mean. Like when I first started out, I could not do a thing as Jantid took my best friend, I kept thinking there had to be something, but after months; I realized that if I had dived in, I would be gone too. Life is funny that way, sometimes you can find a way to help, other times it leaves you with an awful taste that will not go away."

Janice nods as she replies,

"Yeah, I have that bad taste now, it does not taste good."

Jade answers,

"No it does not, that is what sucks, and you were a police officer, so yes I can understand those feelings. All we can do is hope there is not a next time."

Before Janice can respond, a sound of snapping wood, looking towards the other boat as it breaks into pieces. The men nowhere in sight, as the boat begins to disappear. The Jantid's descend back to the depths, as everyone levitates towards the monitor. Watching as they begin going their separate ways and disappear into the darkness. Decisions made to follow one of them. Choosing the one headed towards the shores of Mexico. Following with the camera, once in a while seeing an image as it occasionally rises. The sonar stops beeping after a while, as everyone runs around trying to figure out what happened. Jade decides to lower the camera, turning on the lights, as the camera falls into the depths of eight-hundred feet range. Seeing a little movement, the creature has settled on the bottom.

#21

Three a.m. Jade gets up, and notices the boats upper lights on, creeping up the stairs quietly. Jim is standing outside talking on a satellite phone, with his back to her, he continues to talk. Overhearing a conversation, she is listening to what Jim is talking about,

"…Honestly, I did try! I cannot help you idiots. What the hell was with the antimatter? I told you I would. I am a man of my word. Get off my back and let me do my thing. Okay, bye!"

As Jade slinks back downstairs, Jim comes walking in and stops, quietly putting the phone down after clearing the number. Heading downstairs, running into Jade just coming from the bathroom. Jim surprised, asks,

"Jade! What are you doing up?"

Jade responds,

"Had to go to the bathroom, what are you doing up?"

Jim appears worried, as he answers,

"Same just had a smoke and was going to use the can."

Jade looks at him trying to hold back a new anger, as she replies,

"Okay, goodnight Jim!"

Jim smiles, as he replies,

"Night Jade."

Walking back to her cabin, Jade flicks on her laptop, as it starts up, hearing Jim head to his cabin, and close the door. Jade begins clicking away, sending an e-mail out. Turning it off, Jade lays down, resting, but with one eye open.

Seven a.m. Jade sits up, turns her computer back on, and clicks away again. Hearing noises from the kitchen, she takes a quick look, opens up the file, and closes it once she sees the message. Walking out of her room to where everyone else is, Jade looks at everyone, and making eye contact with everyone before replying annoyed,

"Morning everyone! I have some bad news."

Everyone looks at Jade bewildered, as Jade looks straight-faced, as she begins again,

"This bad news is because of something that happened last night…"

Janice and Rick are first to respond simultaneously,

"What happened?"

Jade looks at everyone again, and replies angrily,

"Well, I received an e-mail this morning, going into great detail about a call that was made from this boat. In this e-mail, it has the detailed conversation…"

Jim begins sweating, and blurts out loudly,

"…Wait! I will admit that was my call. That call sounds bad, but it is not what you think. I swear! I will tell you everything. A couple of months ago, I was approached by this Russian woman. I fell in love with her accent. We ended up in bed together. In the morning, she told me that a man would come talk to me in about an hour. I didn't think anything of it, why should I? Anyway, after she left and this man showed up, I found out he was KGB. He told me my loved ones would be in great harm if I did not do, what they wanted. They want the boat Jade! They know what it can do, they sent those two men to gain your trust, then they were going to kill everyone, I am sure that included me too! I…"

Jade's eyes turn to fire, as she replies angrily,

"…Seriously after all we have been through, you were going to sell us out?"

Jim worried, as everyone stands up cornering him, as he replies,

"Jade, I…"

Jade yells while slamming Jim across the face,

"SHUT UP! You know what these devices are capable of right. Of course, you do! You were there when they briefed us. I brought Janice aboard because of how overworked we all are. I have more trust for her, then I do for you…"

Jim pleadingly responds,

162

Jantid

"…Ja…"

Jade screams even louder,

"SHUT UP! Do not interrupt me again. These devices can kill millions of people with one flick of a switch, but since you pulled your pants down and got yourself some, who cares about the rest of us…RIGHT? You were told, everything here is not to be disclosed to anyone. Let us see, right here and I quote, "Everything is ready for 'your' arrival at three a.m. tomorrow morning, I have sent the global positioning to your coordinates. The creature is very close, if you have rubber bottomed boats, send them, as the creature does not detect this material." End quote, what do you have to say for yourself now?"

Jim tears up, as he pleads,

"I am sorry, to all of you. I had no choice but to help them…"

Jade glares long and hard, as she responds,

"…There is always a choice, I have said that a thousand times. Janice knows what I am talking about, Rick knows what I have said, and you are the only one who thought he was above what I said. You had a choice to continue to help us find a way to rid the waters of these contrived creatures. To help the world become a better place, a safer place. You chose to make a deal with the devil Jim. We are not going to be here when they come, we now have to dock with the carrier, and go back until this mess clears up. Did you think they were not monitoring the boat Jim? They said there would always be someone watching our every move. They approved Janice, but Not Frank the head officer, why, not even I know that. Sorry Jim, you will be placed under arrest. When we get to the undisclosed spot, they will take you in."

Jim shakes his head, as he responds,

"No Jade, please, I cannot go where they are going to send me...please..."

Jade angrily states,

"I am sorry Jim! You knew the rules when you came aboard."

Jim bolts past everyone, as he runs up the stairs, with Jade, Janice, and Rick on his heels. He leaps over the side of the boat into the water, Rick grabs a gaff, and tries to reach Jim, and Jim slaps it away screaming he is never going back, the sonar begins bleeping as Jim swims for the shoreline. The bleeps become rapid, as Janice takes a look at the monitor, a twelve-foot shark is heading towards Jim, who, shortly after disappears in a cloud of red and does not come up again. Jade looks at Janice, and Rick, replying,

"Sorry guys, I had no choice, we cannot let this boat fall into evil hands."

Rick nods, as he replies,

"We know Jade. I just never expected it to be Jim who would betray us! He was on this boat longer then I was."

Janice responds,

"I understand too Jade, I mean if these things do what you have said they can do, and then yeah, I cannot see you had a choice."

Jade shakes her head, as she tries to piece together Jim's actions, as she replies,
"Sad as it was, I thought he would not do that either, he knows what was at stake. Everything, so many lives at stake, and he does that...I

would have given my life for him, and he throws this curve at me, at us. Rick, get us out of here, this is going to set us back weeks, maybe months."

Rick heads to the wheelhouse, as Janice looks at the stressed out Jade, who is covering her face with her hands. Janice speaks in a soft tone,

"You had to do it, you had to call him out, and there was nothing you could do to stop it. As you told me yesterday, you tried to warn them, but they kept coming the same direction, if you wouldn't have done anything, we would all be dead. Your words did say more than you did. I understand, and so should you."

Jade lowers her hands, as she responds,

"You know your right, he brought this on himself, the men involved said explicitly what this would mean if someone else had this boat. I am sure they will talk with you as well Janice. They are not bad people they just have a lot of rules to follow."

Janice smiles, as she replies,

"I know I figured there would be something I would have to commit to."

Jade smiles, as she responds,

"Once we get there, just follow their instructions, and we will be back out here soon! I guess it depends what kind of trouble Jim brought our way?"

Janice nods, as she answers,

"Hopefully not too much. I want to kill this thing and enjoy the beaches again."

Jade nods, as she replies,

"Yes, so do I. enjoy it for a week, no worries at all, just fun and sun?"

#22

Three weeks after Jim took his life, the reminders of what he did still exists. The never-ending questions keep coming in an effort to make sure none of the three members, has revealed anything more. Once Jade, Janice, and Rick docked the boat, everyone's blindfolded and taken for three hours of the darkest travels anyone has ever taken. Once separated from each other, masked men began an onslaught of questions from where everyone met, to up-to-the-minute details of where each person was during a day.

Today, everyone(s) told they will have to stand before the heads of the people who run this secretive program.

Fears seen on the three faces, one of uncertainty. Jade's escorted down a long ominous hallway to a door, into a room filled with voices, and single chair with a bright light over it. Sitting Jade down in the chair, shortly after the door slams a screaming echo of wood on metal. Paper rattles around and pen lights swirl around in the darkness. Finally, a woman speaks in a soft but stern voice,

"Jade Mills…is that correct?"

Jade nods, as she replies,

"Yes, that is my name ma'am."

The woman asks,

"Thank you, I am going to ask a few questions, and you answer them if you can…okay?"

Jade, blinded by the light responds,

"Yes, I will answer any and all questions set before me."

The woman states,

"Great! Looking at these papers, your employment with us for three years, and twenty-six days now. Previously, you were employed by the U.S. Government, and you were one of the first biologists at the original Chernobyl site April 27, 1986. You have always reported to us on time and have never gone rogue on anything asked of you. I have no question about your integrity…that said, what about Janice Tore's? The information we have, says she has very little experience in Biology but has a lengthy police officer background, but is she trustable?"

Jade takes a deep breath, as she replies confidently,

"Yes, Janice was employed as a police officer, she began by helping me/us on the boat. She has never divulged any information about the boat to anyone. She does not have the experience you all expect, but her ideas have helped us forward the plan to destroy this manmade atrocity."

The woman sounds a slight bit happier, as she asks,

"Thank you, Jade, what about Rick Aim's, what about him? He has some of what we look for. He was a dock worker, has a few criminal charges, what do you think about his tractability?"

Jade takes another deep breath, and answers,

"Rick, he was a dockhand, when he joined, he soon became a trusted man, he stays with the boat almost all the time, I have never seen, or found any outgoing calls to anyone, and he has no family ties. I do trust him."

The woman scribbles down something, as she responds,

"Thank you, I know we have held you, and your friends here for quite some time. I do apologize for the inconvenience, but as you know, the people who are in this room, are dedicated to not creating wars. These devices have global implications in the wrong hands. We must be sure this does not happen again. That being said, we want you to continue your search to destroy this creature, I think everyone in this room will agree that you are the best qualified."

A loud thumping of hands on tables. Jade speaks up,

"Thank you all. I am grateful to you all. I will do my best to eliminate this creature…"

As the room quiets down, the woman responds,

"Yes Jade, we have another ship waiting for you. We added a missile of sorts. A torpedo more so, this is a plasma-based weapon, as we know by what you have said, this is the top predator in the ocean at this time. Therefore this weapon will vaporize anything living within a mile radius of the impact. This means you would have to be outside of five thousand eighty feet to ensure your safety. This weapon will take out this creature one hundred percent. Based on everything you have sent us, this is the weapon of choice."

Jade sits in the chair in awe, as she replies,

"Wow, plasma? What happens if we are in that range?"

The woman stays quiet for a moment, then replies,

"Well we have tried to reinforce the ship, but the closer you are, the less likely you will survive. You can lock on to it from a distance away, but the further away you are from the moving target, the less likely you will get a direct hit. To get the most accurate hit, you must be closer, and try and get to the safe zone before firing that is all I can suggest. I know it's not ideal, but that is what we have for you, Jade."

Jade ponders the options and replies,

"Alright, I guess those odds will have to do, if we want to destroy it…wait, what about the Nitrogen that stopped it dead?"

The woman pauses, as she whispers amongst the others. A few minutes later, she responds,

"Yes, we tried to make a nitrogen-based weapon, it failed, between the depths and recovering time, this creature would be back alive before anyone could get down there. At seventy feet, it works, but you would have to break through ice, before getting to the creature, that still leaves it time to reanimate. Without going nuclear, this plasma weapon is the best choice. Oh, yes, before it slips my mind, our sources say that was an American submarine, the U.S.S. Great White which blew up. The cause is unknown to us as of yet. Our intel makes it sound like a power failure was the reason, but we will know more once they recover the sub itself."

Jade nods, as she answers,

"Okay, I see, can we use the Nitrogen on the surface level, for the tentacles?"

The woman answers intrigued,

"Yes, that is a good idea! We will add nitrogen guns in the event of it grabbing on. Thank you, Jade. You may get ready to depart with your crew after we install these weapons. Thank you for answering our questions."

#23

Another nine days waiting, as the guns are hidden from plain sight. All Jade can do is watch. Finally, these people disembark from Jade's ship.

Jade, Janice, and Rick are finally sailing in the open ocean once again. The sunshine is as bright as ever, the blue ocean is calm. Everybody goes about their jobs, nobody wants to talk about their experiences. As the day dredges on, an uneasy feeling, seen on each of their faces. Finally, Jade has enough, as she responds,

"Alright everyone, we have to talk about this. I know we went through heck there. Let us get this out in the open, so we can get Jantid! Rick?"

Rick replies,

"Umm, okay, I know this is the way they run things, but over three weeks, I answered so many questions it was ridiculous."

Jade nods, as she answers,

"Yes, Rick...remember though, we have never had anyone ever disclose so much information about that boat before. Jim almost got us killed, over that boat, given to people who were surely going to put those weapons to use. We are still together, that is a positive. They would not have us together if they believed anyone of us were going to turn around and do what Jim did."

Rick nods, as he seems to understand, and replies,

"Yes, I guess that makes sense Jade."

Jade turns to Janice, and asks,

"What about you Janice? I know your police training probably came in handy back there."

Janice nods, as she responds,

"Yes, but it was not as bad as it first seemed. They grilled me, but not in a menacing way, I could see they just wanted answers about each of you, so I told them what I thought. They were happy enough after that."

Jade nods, as she answers,

"Yes, that sounds about right. No matter what we think, they have our best interests in mind. They just need to know we have their backs as well."

Seeing everyone ease up, they start becoming the friends they were before the incident, smiles begin taking form, as the three friends sit there, and chat about everything. As the day passes on into night everyone settles down. The day ends on a great note.

At first light, everyone comes up to the wheelhouse, a constant beeping coming from the sonar has everyone running hurriedly. Looking as images, (large) ones appear. Jade looks at Rick, and responds,

"Can you get a camera down there? Something is not right here?"

Rick smiles, as he replies,

"You got it."

Rick runs to the stern and begins fiddling with the case holding the cameras. Finally dropping the camera in the water. Rick yells out,

"Is that deep enough?"

Jade shouts back quickly,

"Keep going, another fifty feet. Right there."

Rick comes running in after he locks it down, the three of them watch, as Jantids of all sizes seem to be heading the same way. Jade shockingly states,

"We need to follow them. I did not even realize there are that many of them. Look at them all, hundreds of them."

Jantid

#24

Three days into following this horde of Jantids, Jade had fuel boats come to their position. As Jade, Janice, and Rick head towards the Cayman Islands. The sonar is constantly bleeping away, as the numbers of Jantids grow into thousands covering a few square miles. The plans keep changing over the hours, as more keep coming from the deep. Watching sharks, whales, and dolphins swim, as if the Jantids are not there. An unusual twist compared to months earlier when they would have been speeding in the opposite direction. Jade glances over at the others, as she confusingly asks,

"Why aren't the sharks swimming away from the Jantid's like before?"

Rick and Janice stare blankly at the screen, looking for an answer to give Jade. Finally, Janice responds,

"Perhaps, Jantid is evolving? Something the other animals can't detect yet?"

Jade nods agreeing, as Rick does as well. After a few more minutes pass Jade finally answers,

"Yes, perhaps you're right. Watching sharks pass by within mere feet of the horde of Jantid's. Not a single flinch, or attempt to scurry away from them. Let's continue to watch, maybe we'll catch an idea of what's happening down there?"

The camera in the water still recording the masses, Jade watching closely. The monitor showing the Jantids swimming erratically, especially the big ones. Like they are drunk, bumping into smaller ones. They all come to rest at the bottom, no more than a mile off the shoreline, on a shelf about five hundred feet down. The boat comes to a stop close by…but not to close. Throughout the day, more Jantids come and rest on the bottom. Jade, Janice, and Rick sit around the monitor, trying to figure out what is going on, Jade finally speaks up,

"This is new? Smaller fish are swimming around the Jantid's, not a care in the world, why?"

Janice ponders for a moment, as she watches. Soon she responds,

"Something with the way those large ones are swimming erratically? I do not know if Rick agrees with me or not?"

Rick answers,

"I do not really know? I would say they are in a trance of some sort, maybe mating?"

Jade looks at them both, and answers,

"That could be Rick, perhaps we should wait until they stop coming, then hit them with the plasma torpedo."

Rick quickly answers,

"I honestly think we should hit them now! Kill them all before they begin to leave. What do you think Janice?"

Janice sits watching the monitor, as she replies,

"I would wait. See what they are up to first. If any get away, it would be nice to know if this is their hotspot or just a place they stop on their way to somewhere else?"

Jade smiles, and answers,

"Yes, good point Janice lets learn a little bit more about them, just in case."

As they continue to discuss what to do, something hits the boat, taking out the camera. As everyone gets up to see what it is that hit the boat, seeing a greyish colored weird shaped creature. Rick rushes to get another camera ready to deploy into the water a grey substance is floating nearby the boat. As the camera is set at fifty feet to prevent the loss of this camera. Everyone rushes in to watch the monitor. The water is too murky to see anything. Rick goes to move the camera even lower, there is nothing but murkiness seen. Bringing the camera back up and into the boat, the camera covered with this greyish substance. Janice, and jade grabbing some specimen cups. Placing some of this liquid into the cups, and wiping down the camera and putting it away. Half-hour later, the water is still murky, as Jade comes back with the finding of the murky substance, she shakes her head, and replies,

"I thought it was one thing, I am wrong, but I know what it is…decaying flesh! Before you say anything, from what I can see, they would be mutating again, my best guess is that is why the sharks and other fish did not recognize their signatures."

Janice, and Rick both look confused, as Janice replies,

"How is this possible Jade?"

Jade looks at them closely, as she responds,

"This is a guess Janice, Rick, but I believe from what I saw they cannot grow, they are more like a snake, and they have to shed their skin. By the way, that decaying skin is changing. I believe they will be a new species after the change."

Rick worriedly replies,

"What kind of species are we talking about Jade?"

Jade shakes her head, and answers,

"I do not know Rick, but they are losing those transparent tentacles. That is what is decaying in the water."

Janice responds,

"That is how they sense their victims is it not?"

Jade nods, and answers,

"That is what I believed to Janice, but I am not sure now? If that other one was not in pieces, perhaps we could have seen into it better?"

Rick looks confused, as he asks,

"So what do we do now Jade? Kill it, or wait to see what it becomes?"

Jade looks stressed, as she tries to assess this whole new possible ball game scenario. She answers,

"I do not know Rick? If we kill them, and any get away, we will be chasing another species, if we wait too long, they may all escape. I don't know?"

As everyone contemplates the situation, the waters below begin to thrash around, like a fight going on. As everyone runs to the bow, looking over the side, the murkiness prevents anyone from seeing anything that is happening below. They all make the decision to lock in on the area, and head back a mile, and release the bomb. Hoping that clears out this species of manmade hell for the last time. As the boat motor starts and begins reversing, something latches on, and the boat is not moving anywhere. Hoping to power through, it's no use, the boat is stuck in the water. After ten minutes of trying, it is apparent the boat is not going anywhere. Everyone heads down to the galley to grab a bite to eat and discuss the new dreaded ideas that are about to play out. Sitting there waiting for each other to say the words everyone knows is coming, but none wants to be the one to say them. Jade finally gets sick of the silence, clearing her throat of the menacing lump in her throat, as she is trying to speak,

"I, umm, I guess we all know what the outcome of this is going to be now. I guess poking the dragon once too often gets you into incredible situations. I truly am glad to know both of you. You truly are my friends. I want you to know, you both are my family. I know what this weapon is capable of, and the damage to anything in the zone, at a five hundred foot depth, there is no way of surviving this."

Janice clears her throat, as she replies,

"Perhaps we should see about waiting it out, they haven't sunk us yet...could be mistaken on what it grabbed?"

Jade nods, as she responds,

"That is possible Janice. We will try a few more times before saying, that's the last time. I figure if I wait to say these things to you two, by then it will be too late."

Rick looks at them both, and states,

"Yes, I feel the same way, but if we are going to lose, I am glad it is with you two Jade, Janice."

Before anyone can say anything, a boats horn blow, catching everyone's attention. Looking up, a cruise ship coming towards the Island. Jade looks at Rick, and Janice, before shouting,

"Shit! That ship is heading this way, try to contact them, get them the hell away from here."

Rick grabs the radio, and begins talking,

"Cruise Liner headed for the Cayman Islands; change your course by one point five degrees east…copy?"

Flipping channels and repeating the message to the ship, who is not answering on any channel? Jade gets that disheartened look on her face turning to look at the ship coming, and Janice, and Rick. Placing her hand on her temples, and running them through her hair, looking at both of them before answering,

"I want you off this boat now!"

Janice looks shocked, as she responds,

"Jade, no…I am staying with you…"

Jade looks angrier than ever, as she shouts,

Jantid

"NO! Take one of the Nitrogen surface guns, and get off this boat!"

Rick doesn't know what to say, as Janice responds,

"Why what happened? Why are you saying this Jade? We can still get out of here."

Jade grabs both Rick, and Janice's hands, and replies,

"Janice, you are my friend, but we are not going anywhere. See that flashing light, that means there are holes in the ship, we are sinking. I am not going to argue with either of you. Get into that dingy, and get out of here. That ship is going to be in range of the one-mile zone in a matter of half hour minimally, get to the Island, at full speed you should be on land in five minutes…GO!"

The angered look on Jade's face gets Janice, and Rick, on the fast track to getting the dingy ready to go, grabbing a Nitrogen gun, and placing in the boat. Hoping in, they begin to lower it as Jade stands there looking at the instrument control panel, flicking switches. As the dingy begins a path to the Island and slowly starts getting smaller. Jade sits in the Captain's chair, watching the lights going off in their various stages of urgently. Jade glares at the monitor, as she shouts,

"Goddamn you Jantid, you finally got me. Over ten years, I have been chasing you from Russia to here. You and your little family are finally going to pay!"

Grabbing the binoculars, seeing Janice, and Rick getting help onto another boat heading towards Mexico. Smiling, Jade whispers,

"Good, I love you guys! I will meet you two again, one day."

Tears filling Jade's eyes, as she stands up, and walks over to a red box, opening it up revealing a panel with a targeting system. Flicking switches, and pointing the targeting arrows one point two degrees in from of the boat at five hundred feet. As the calculating begins, the machine turns red, and hums, as Jade responds,

"This dead man's song is horrible coming from this thing. Everything's targeted!"

Everything is lining up, looking to see how far Janice and Rick are, and switching to the cruise ship. The system speaks.

"Attention Jade! The dense mass you have chosen to target will be in optimum range in thirty seconds. Safety range from blast will not be able to be reached at this time…consider reallocating aiming range, or resetting timer:"

Jade looks at the speaker, as she shouts,

"Shut up!"

Placing her hand on the button, as the timer reaches zero, pressing it, and loud siren sounds. The machine speaks again.

"The torpedo is two minutes from destination…be advised the blast will affect one square mile. There is a ship approaching this range, appears to be a cruise liner…"

Flicking the volume off, Jade looks towards the ship that is still on its current course, looking back at the system, as it shows the depth of the torpedo. Jade sits back down, holding her cup of coffee, tears streaming down her cheeks, her head falling lower. Watching the torpedo getting closer to the mass. Taking a deep breathe, taking a sip of coffee, standing up walking out onto the deck…

Jantid

Rick and Janice watch, as the cruise liner has ignored every attempt to contact them. Looking through a pair of binoculars, Janice sees Jade standing at the stern of the boat. Not seeing more than just a little figure, just as Janice lowers the binoculars… (Boom) the waters near Jade's boat turn an intense white with blue swirls as a tidal wave forty feet high makes its way towards Janice, Rick, and the cruise liner. Watching as the wave hits the cruise liner, bolts of lightning creeping around the ship, as the wave passes by. As the wave approaches the boat, Janice, along with everyone else braces for the worst. Watching as the wave begins to slow, and falls, going from a tidal wave to an eight-foot white cap. As the boat begins to nosedive, and comes back to bobbing in the water, as they make their way back to Mexico. Rick and Janice just look at each other, as tears begin filling their eyes.

#25

A week after the explosion that took the life of Jade Mills, services held with only Janice, and Rick attending. Sitting there looking at each other in (disbelief) of what happened. The authorities continue to investigate what happened, as thirty-nine people died on the cruise liner from their pacemakers exploding in their chests. A small chunk of the Cayman Islands destroyed by this weapon. Officials picking pieces of something unknown but rather smelly out of the waters. The Cayman Island resort is closed until this unknown stench is gone. Janice and Rick head to the hotel to have a drink in honor of Jade. As they walk in and sit down, a loud-voiced man comes sits down at the table next to them. As their drinks come, the man flings his arm and knocks the drink in Janice's lap. The man looks, and laughs, as Janice responds,

"What the hell!"

The man laughs, as he responds,

"Don't worry sweetie, it looks good on you. Ha-ha!"

The fire in Janice's eyes, as she grabs the man's drink, as he now looks pissed, and she dumps it in his face and replies,

"Huh, don't do a thing for your looks!"

The man yells,

"Why you bitch!"

Janice punches the man in the face, sending him flying to the floor. The man grabs his jaw replying,

"What, that time of the month for you?"

Janice replies,

"No! You are a disrespectful piece of shit…"

Everyone cheers, claps, and a voice out of the crowd responds,

"Good! Now maybe people can enjoy themselves, you asshole!"

As security comes in and escorts the man away to the cheers of the whole bar. A waiter brings them three drinks replying,

"These are from those people over there."

The two men and woman raise their glasses, Janice, and Rick pick up two of the drinks, and raise them back, as they all smile and go back to their own conversations. Janice turns to Rick and replies,

"To Jade, a great woman no matter what happened! A friend, who did what she could, sacrificed her life for ours! This drink is so you can join us one last time."

Rick wipes his eyes, as he responds,

"Yes, a drink for a great woman indeed, saved our lives in order to kill Jantid! You Jade, you were not selfish, and you knew what you were going to do. To you, my friend!"

Janice replies,

"Yes to you!"

Clinking the glasses together, and drinking both down. A man standing there, pipes up, and responds,

"Was she the one involved in that horrible explosion?"

Janice smiles slightly, as she nods, and replies,

"Yes she was, she saved countless lives, and what is worse, no one will ever know how close they were to dying."

The man asks concerned,

"Oh…why, what happened?"

Rick looks at him, and responds,

"A monster!"

The man looks confused, as he answers,

"I don't get it? What kind of monster?"

Janice replies,

"The kind that makes you never want to go into the ocean again kind of monster."

Jantid

Shaking his head, Janice, and Rick watch as he disappears into the crowd. Janice and Rick discuss their futures, Rick says he is going to stay in Mexico. Janice states she's going to Canada, to be with her sister who lives in Saskatoon. As they leave, they hug each other one last time, Rick heads into the hotel. Janice begins walking towards the airport. Along the way, Frank Jorden pulls up beside her and stops. Getting out, he responds,

"Janice! Hey Janice!"

Janice just glares at him, as she snaps back,

"What?"

Frank looks sorrowful, as he replies,

"I just want to say, I am sorry for what happened…"

Janice gives him the coldest stare, as she answers,

"Best thing that could've happened!"

Frank quickly replies confused,

"What do you mean? The chief told me, I could hire you back. That is great news."

Janice rolls her eyes, as she states,

"For you perhaps Frank, that is not my life anymore…"

Frank looks shocked, as he responds,

"What do you mean 'not for you' you lived for the job?"

Janice nods with that cold stare fixed onto Frank, as she replies,

"I did, once. I want to enjoy my life, away from this here. I am going to make a new start elsewhere. Somewhere I can be me, and not get scrutinized by people who I thought were friends."

Frank cautiously responds,

"Janice, I had no choice…"

Janice shakes her head, as she answers angrily,

"As an old friend once told me, you always have a choice, but sometimes the choice you want, and need are two entirely different components. The right choice is usually the hardest one to make. That is why this is my choice. Leaving behind everything, I have ever known. Goodbye, Frank."

Frank shakes his head, as he states,

"That is a poor choice Janice; you know you belong here with friends."

Janice grins a little, as she replies,

"No Frank, that is where you are wrong, I have few friends here. After what the police department pulled, I know I have even fewer friends here now."

As Frank continues, Janice walks away into the setting sun of a new future.

Jantid

#26

May 27, 1997, noon. Janice walks into her sister's house, as Maria stops her at the front door, and states,

"Wait, before you go inside, there is something waiting for you on the couch."

Janice looks confused, as she replies,

"Okay? What is it?"

Maria smiles, and responds,

"That is for you to find out."

Maria walks out the door, leaving Janice to ponder the 'what?' As Janice makes her way around the corner, seeing purple hair. Stopping! Thinking for a moment before running to see if that hair belongs to who she thinks it is. Janice responds,

"Oh my God, it's you, but how?"

Jade turns to look at Janice and replies,

"Hi Janice, long time."

Janice almost falls on the ground, but catches herself on the couch, as she responds confused,

"Yes, way too long, am I glad to see you. How did you escape, I saw the explosion."

Jade smiles, as she responds,

"That still dumbfounds me to this day, Janice. I was standing on the deck. Knowing that torpedo was mere seconds away, as that stupid thing kept informing me. I stood there on the deck, it occurred to me, that plasma is energy based. I took off every piece of jewelry I was wearing, including my bra, anything with a metal base in it. I wrapped myself in that rubber mat on the back deck, I pulled the inflatable raft cord, I was just about to step into the raft when (Boom!) Next thing I see, I am about forty or fifty feet above the water, our boat disintegrated in a second, nothing left. I watched as the electrical charge blew through the water killing everything in its path."

Jade stands up, and hugs Janice, as she continues talking,

"I saw the boat you and Rick were riding in. Last thing I remember is hitting the water, feeling the tingles like a massive belly flop. I woke up in the life raft. I am not sure how I got in? I know my leg was broken in two places my left arm was shattered. Spent the next four weeks in the hospital, once my casts were off, I went searching for Jantid, either he is scared off, or we killed them, I don't know? I searched for Rick, I found him, and he said you moved to Saskatoon Canada. So after I had everything in order, I came here."

Janice's smile grows to epic proportions, as she replies,

"Oh my God, that is awesome…not what you went through, but that you are alive and here. I was so heartbroken of what I thought happened…"

Jade smiles, as she replies,

"You don't have to worry about that anymore Janice. I was talking with your sister, she said the basement suite is for rent, and I thought since I have no idea how to find anything in this city…"

Janice shouts,

"Yes!"

Jade looks at Janice, stating,

"Yes, what? I have not said anything…"

Janice shakes her head, as she responds excitedly,

"Yes you did, you said you are going to stay here."

Jade smiles, as she answers,

"Janice, you read people too well, must be the police officer in you! Yeah, this will take some getting used to, but I am done chasing after man's mistakes. After that close encounter with death, before I came to Mexico, I would not give it a second thought, but you and Rick definitely showed true friendship. Something looking for a killer does not give you, friends, enemies by the dozen, but not friends, or friendship!"

Janice can't stop smiling, as she replies,

"Yes, Jade, oh I missed you…"

Janice flings herself at Jade again, hugging her as tight as she can, whispering,

"I am never letting you go again."

www.ingramcontent.com/pod-product-compliance
Lightning Source LLC
Chambersburg PA
CBHW020609250626
47154CB00004B/1424